CHI-TOWN BOSSES & THE WOMEN THAT LOVE EM 4

ANNA BLACK

❦ I ❦

GEMMA (GEM) JACKSON

I dabbed my eyes as I watched Chas and Rel exchange vows. Everything was so beautiful, and I thought back on the day that Chas exchanged vows with Chris. I was a lot younger then and definitely wasn't a bridesmaid, plus I was too young to remember a lot of the details of her horrible marriage. I was only fourteen or fifteen back then, and I remember saying *goodbye* to my big sister Gabby at the airport when she went to be with that asshole Mario. Well back then, no one thought he was an asshole, but that pretty much describes his stupid ass now. Hell, the way Mario treated and cheated on my sister, I can't stand to see his ass. When he was home on leave for the holiday's year before last, he knew damn well not to say one muthafuckin' word to me when he saw me at church. Yes, we were in the house of God, but that didn't stop me from giving him my mani-cured middle finger when he looked in my direction.

Yes, I knew I was wrong when I did it and hoped no one else saw me, but he was one of my least favorite persons, and I was so happy that my sister wised up and left his dumb ass in Texas. Thinking back on all the tears she cried on that long drive back to the Chi makes me cringe at times, but as I looked at my brother-in-law, Gutta, standing next to Rel, I smiled because he was so good to Gabby. He adored her and my little niece, and for a nigga to kill for you, that was love. Although I never said it out loud or even asked, I knew my brother-in-law found a way to cancel that crazy bitch; and even if I had substantial evidence, I'd take that shit to my grave because we all wanted that bitch dead. If I had a way of doing it without going to prison, I would have; shit, that is just how much I loved my damn sisters. Gabby and Gracie were not only my sisters, but they were also my best friends, and I was so fucking happy that they had found Gutta and Malice.

"I will," Chas sniffled, and I dabbed my eyes again. I was so happy for my girlfriend Chas because, from all the horror stories that I had heard when I was old enough to listen to them, Chris' ass should have suffered longer than just a couple of bullets to his damn chest. Harsh, I know, but hey, I didn't have much sympathy for muthafuckas like Trina, Silky, and Chris. I mean, what they had done to my girl and fam was disturbing, and I was glad all of them bitches were roasting in hell.

"You may kiss your new bride," the minister said, and the church applauded. He presented the new couple, and then they jumped the broom. I thought it was a lovely traditional touch, but if and when I get married, it would not be in a church with all of these damn flowers and candles and shit. I was going to Vegas. I wasn't into all of the girly wedding dreams and spending a grip on a damn dress that you would only wear once and for a few hours was the dumbest shit I've ever heard of but to each his own.

When we started to file out, I locked arms with Royal's annoying ass. I tried to keep my eyes off of him during the ceremony, and I wanted so bad to switch with Stephanie because Rel's friend Drew was fine as fuck. I mean, my sisters and Chas and even Tori somehow saw this *match made in heaven* for Royal and I, but this dude, let me tell you, he was just so arrogant and so damn, damn, damn... like me. Yes, I will fucking admit it! He was *too* much like me, and I couldn't be with me. I mean, it's so damn annoying how he never let me get the last word, or how he always had a quick comeback. I never thought I'd meet my match until I met his ass. And fuck! I didn't want to like him, so this being nice to me, bullshit was getting on my last nerve.

"All the bridal party, come this way for a few more photos," the coordinator yelled. "Chas and Rel, this way for the receiving line and after a few more photos, we will head out to the cars and head over to the reception," she continued as her workers guided us into another room that I referred to as the holding room because that was where we were held up before the wedding. I was so shocked that we'd be taking more photos since we had taken so many before the wedding; but I then recalled, it was only of the women, none with the men.

"So, what you got going on after the reception?" Royal asked.

I did my best not to roll my eyes and then replied, "Home. I have a shift in the morning."

"On a Saturday?" he quizzed.

"Yes, I didn't get married, and since I took today off for the wedding, I have to work tomorrow," I said.

"Okay then, tomorrow evening after work?"

"Why?" I shot him.

"I thought maybe you and I can grab some dinner or Netflix and chill," he said, giving me that sexy ass grin that I could not stand. He was a younger, much slimmer version of his brothers, and his cocky ass attitude drove me insane.

"Umm, no. I don't fuckin' Netflix and chill, that is some old cheap ass nigga hook-up. Besides, I am watching Gianna for Gab and Gutta, they are doing their Valentine thing tomorrow since the wedding was today."

"Even better. I can help you watch the baby. She is my niece, too," he added.

"True, but I'm good, and I don't need any help watching my niece."

"You sure because I'm free. I mean, I can swing by and help you change them diapers."

"What you know about changing diapers?" I frowned.

He chuckled. "Not a damn thing, but for you, I'd learn."

I tried to hold in my smile. Royal was charming enough, but I needed a man that I could push around and control. Royal was too much like his brothers, too assertive for me, and he and I would always bump heads. "Thanks for the offer, but I am good," I said and walked away. I hurried over to Grace and interrupted her and Malice. I didn't care what they were talking about, but I wanted to get away from Royal's ass. Before long, we were back in the sanctuary taking more pictures. Rel and Chas had a long ass truck of some sort that the bridal party would ride in to get to the reception. When we got in, Royal quickly took a seat next to me, and everyone was getting in so fast, I couldn't move. Gutta and Gabby had their own car take them, and Tori decided to ride with her husband. It was me, Malice, Grace, Stephanie, Drew, Crystal, Rel's other friend Damon, and Pain In My Royal Ass.

He slid his arm around me, and I rolled my eyes. I looked at Grace, and she mouthed the words, *be nice Gloria Jean Jr.*, and I wanted to give her the finger, but I declined on that. The guys started popping bottles and pouring and passing glasses around. I wondered what was taking so long for the driver to get his ass in so we can roll because I wanted to get out of this damn vehicle and get as far away from Royal as I could.

Drew handed me a glass, "Thanks," I said, giving him a bright smile.

"You are welcome, beautiful," he smiled back.

"Slow your roll, Drew, she wit me," Royal said, and I almost spit out my drink.

"No, I'm not," I disputed.

He just looked at Drew. "Like I said," Royal declared, and Drew looked the other way.

I looked at Royal and spoke between clenched teeth. "The fuck Royal?!"

"Relax baby and drink your drink, you are not going to resist me forever."

"We shall see," I snapped back, and then the driver finally got in. He turned on the music, and we had a good time, drinking, laughing, and talking all kinds of shit on our forty-minute ride to the reception hall. Once we made it, we all hurried inside because it was still fucking cold, and none of us wore coats. The coordinator was there to line us up so we could make our entrance and get to the bridal table. There I was arm and arm with baby Royal again. I wasn't sure if it was because I had drunk the champagne on a fairly empty stomach, but his touch didn't irritate me like it had before. Once we were all at the table, the DJ announced Rel & Chas, and they both came in wearing different clothing, and I had no idea Chas had plans to change. She was in a tight-fitting red dress, and he was in a black linen pants suit. They looked so beautiful together, and I stood applauding for them and was truly happy for Chas. After we were seated and after the bride and groom danced their first dance, it was time to eat. I was glad the women were on one side and the men on the other, but that didn't stop Royal from eyeing me.

The food was delicious, and our glasses stayed full; and before long, I was in Royal's arms on the dance floor. Yeah, after a few glasses of the bubbly, I loosened up and stop playing him to the left. I had a good time with him and my sisters. That night when the car took us to Gabby's, where Gutta had arranged a car for all of us to get home, Royal asked me to go home with him. I reminded him that I still had work the next morning, so he let me go after he kissed my lips. I should have backed away. My insides were screaming *back away*, but my body stayed pressed against his, and it felt so nice to be in his arms. The kiss was delicious, and I hated that I enjoyed it so much, so I pulled away. He smiled at me, and I let my lips curl up into a smile back at him. He helped me into the back of the car and closed my door. I got home a little close to one, and I was tipsy and knew work wasn't going to happen. I grabbed my cell, texted my co-worker Sonia, and asked her to please switch days with me. She replied, "no problem," and I thanked the heavens and then peeled away my red dress and shoes and didn't bother to clean the makeup from my face. I crawled into bed, and I was sleeping within minutes.

2

RAPHAEL (ROYAL) WILKERSON

I sat in the back of the full-sized SUV, thinking I should have just gotten into my whip and driven myself. Gutta was so paranoid; he thought driving after the evening we had at the reception was a fuck no, so he insisted we all get home in the cars he had ordered for us. I wanted to tell my big bro I was cool, but Gutter was like my hero, and I looked up to my brother. And if he thought it was safer for me and my fam to get transported, I just went with the flow. I smiled and rubbed my palms together when I thought about the kiss that I planted on Gemma's sweet soft lips. Yep, she was feisty and a damn handful, but I could handle her and tame her ass; but to be honest, I like that about her. I wanted a woman who could stand up to me and not just put up with my shit because I didn't come across women like her often. Most bitches were just some old thirsty ass hoes who saw my twenty-six-years-old ass with a business, nice ride, decked out crib, and thought they had hit like on one of them slots in Vegas, but I didn't have no love for broke down bitches that wasn't taking care of themselves.

I mean, don't get me wrong, I'd break my lady off a few stacks, wine and dine her, but I didn't want to carry her. Not in a dating or girlfriend-boyfriend situation. There was a difference between struggling and ain't doing shit than struggling when you are hustling. Some bitches that I came across rolled up in luxury ass cars, not a strand of hair out of place, face beat, and designer down, but live in a fucking roach motel with crates and shit for furniture. This one chick I had hooked up with was rolling around in a nice fucking ass Land Rover, but the bitch had a box spring and mattress on the floor and not even one damn dresser for her damn clothes that were in plastic containers along the wall of her bedroom. I mean, that shit was mind-blowing, so I made a rule. If I met a bad bitch with a nice ride and designer down, I'd ask for an address. Not that I needed that shit in our records because you paid for service before it was done at my detail shops, but just to see where she lived. If it were a reasonably decent or upscale neighborhood, I'd holla; but if I knew I would never go to her hood after dark, *fuck that ho'* no matter how bad she was. I mean, I had met plenty of women at my detailing shops, at Passions, and not one gave me hell like Gemma fucking Jackson.

That little firecracker made my dick hard, and a verbal match with her ass was like foreplay to me, and I had to find a way to romance this woman. I mean, she was just so damn mean, but that shit did not detour me from my pursuit, and I now wanted what my brothers had. I mean, it was like we used to hang long and strong before Gabby, Chas, and Gracie. Those women came along and just took my brothers away, so I had to find me a woman too, and the only woman I finally truly desired was Gemma. I got home, and my two-bedroom townhouse was super quiet, as always. It was stark, barely decorated, because I had no skills in that department. I had the essentials, nothing basic because I didn't take the cheap route, but a woman's touch would have been nice.

Most everything was basic black, gray, red, and white, as simple as could be. I did have a king-sized bed, though, and it was one of those fancy soft headboards because my mom had picked it out. Large eighty-inch screen, oversized sectional, coffee table, and two end tables were in my living room. On my lower level, I had a pool table, bar, armless chairs, and another big screen. When I wasn't with my brothers, I hung with a few of my employees and my boy Tas at my crib, but I rarely brought chicks to my place. I hadn't had anyone steady, so I'd get a room in a heartbeat. I had one girl that used to show up unannounced for about six months straight, and once I finally shook her stalking ass, I stopped bringing randoms home. After the shit my big bro Gutta went through with Trina, I knew I'd never let another woman other than Gemma in my house. I mean, I knew deep down that Gutta wiped that bitch out, but that was something none of us spoke of, and to be painfully fucking honest, I was glad he had. I had scoped that bitch in different places I went, and I was like "brah, that bitch is unstable as fuck." Gutta would nod and assure me he had it under control, and when that bitch was finally on the local news, I smiled because she got what the fuck she deserved.

Ruthless, I know, but some bitches, especially crazy bitches like Trina, would force your hand, and I hoped that my relationship with Gemma didn't lead to anything tragic like it had for my brothers. I mean, I was like fuck, three dead muthafuckas since my family hooked up with their women. Nah, keep that shit, but Gemma, oh my God, Gemma pretty ass Gemma. She was sexy as fuck with a nice lil body on her short ass. Fucking hazel eyes, pretty short hair, and her taper was never overgrown. Her waist was slim, ass plump as fuck, and tits just a handful enough. She favored Grace a lot more than Gab to me, although they looked like fucking triplets; but I think it was those light ass eyes that made her resemble Grace more. Grace had even more luminous eyes but with a mixture of black speckles. Definitely like a damn cat, but nonetheless, the Jackson sisters were gorgeous. Even though Grace was chubby as hell in my opinion, she still looked good and looked good on my brethren's arm. I just wanted what my brothers had at that point. Chas was a beautiful sister too, and Rel was always the most chill and laid back one, but watching him at the reception dancing, laughing, and enjoying his new bride let me see my big bro a little differently. I mean, I knew they were fucking old, but they were happy, and I figured, why not experience what they have now?

I showered, and even though I had plenty to eat, I had danced that shit off. I was six-one, but the slimmest of the four of us, and I inherited my father's slender build. I was cut, worked out daily, but no matter what I ate, I was not as big as Rel and Gutta; and none of us would ever get as big as Malice's *swole* ass. My big brother was a damn beast. I heated up some leftover pizza I had and cracked open a beer.

It was late, and I wished I had Gemma's number. It was too late to call; I knew she had to work the next morning, but I'd text her if I could.

After I finished my pizza and beer, I settled on the sofa and turned on the tube. The next day, I'd get up, check on my shops, and then make sure I go by Gutta's to help babysit my niece. I fell asleep watching ESPN, and then the next day, I woke up close to noon. I dressed, went to check on business, and then called my big brother.

"Wat up, Royal?" he answered.

"Hey, big bro, what's good?" I returned.

"Life, baby, life. Life is all good at casa de Wilkerson. Got big plans for me and the wifey this evening, so it's all good, baby boi."

"Dat's wat's up, what time are y'all heading out? Heard Gemma watching my niece."

"She is and supposed to be by our house by six and she staying overnight. We got a room downtown, and yo' big bro might make Gianna a little brother or sister tonight."

"TMI, big bro, damn. I just wanted to know so I can swing by. You know I am on a mission to get yo' wife's baby sis, right?"

"I do, and good luck with that. According to Gab, Gemma doesn't want your arrogant ass," he said.

"Nonsense. I kissed her last night, so I know I got a chance."

"I see, lil bro. And all this time, I thought that you didn't inherit the Wilkerson's charm gene."

"Ha, ha, ha, big bro. You are wrong, I am my father's son, so y'all better recognize."

"Hey, we know that you are our baby bro, but none of us are as arrogant as you, and maybe, just maybe, Gemma will bring yo' ass down a couple of notches."

"Bro, as bad as I want that, I'd change my religion."

"Damn, good thing for you she is Christian like us, so I wish you luck, baby bro. Gemma is tough, nothing like Gab and Grace."

"And ya' boi got this."

"Well, we are out of the house by six, so do your thang. Just make sure y'all take care of my baby girl. And no fucking around in my damn bed, man. We have three spare bedrooms for that shit." My brother said sternly like he was giving the house rules to a teenager.

"No worries, bro. My niece is good as gold. Plus, Gemma and I ain't nowhere near there yet," I clarified. We had just shared a kiss.

"Say no more, lil bro."

"Aw'ight, enjoy yo' night away with Gab, see yo' ass lata," I said.

"Lata," he said and ended the call. I headed back to my place and chilled for a while. I left out about six, got pizza, and then went straight to my brother's house. I rang the bell, and when she opened the door, I wore a huge smile. "Hey baby, you hungry?"

3

GEMMA

When I looked at the camera and saw Royal, I started not to even go to the damn door, but that damn kiss. That muthafuckin' kiss made me hurry to the door to let his ass in. I opened it, and his cologne and the scent of the pizza hit my nose at once. I started to take the pizza and dismiss his ass, but then I said, "Really, Royal, pizza?"

"Shiiiidddd, this fire is from Fox's Pizza. Not far from my parents. I grew up on this shit, and it is the most mouth-watering pizza on the southside of Chicago."

I giggled. "Well, it is obvious that your ass doesn't get out much because Connie's is my shit," I said, stepping aside. It was a chilly night, and the draft coming inside was too much, and I wanted to close the door.

He stepped in. "Well, unfortunately for Gutta and Gab, they live so damn far, so it is no longer piping hot. We will have to heat it up."

I shut the door. "I am good with that, but you should have called first. What if I had invited someone else to keep me company while I sit with Gianna?"

"His ass would have been a muthafuckin' third wheel because this is my brother's home, not yo' shit, and I am more welcomed than some lame ass nobody that you think you might wanna kick it with," he said, and I followed him into the kitchen. I realized that Gutta and Gabby's spot was not foreign to him, and he knew his way around, just like I did.

"Are you always this fuckin' annoying? I mean, you think the sun rises and sets on yo' ass," I shot.

He put the pizza down onto the island and snickered. He pulled away his leather jacket and then put it on the back of one of the stools at the island. "Well, actually it does in my world, and I think anyone that doesn't think that about themselves has self-esteem issues for real, for real. Like if you don't think you are *the shit*, who else will?" he said.

"I hate to admit that you are right, and even if no one else thinks I'm the shit, fuck 'em."

"You are speaking my language, baby. Let me preheat this oven, grab a cookie sheet, and while we wait for this pizza to warm up, I can love on my niece."

"Well, lucky for you, she is still awake. I have her in the middle of the sectional because this lil chick is rolling over already."

He washed his hands and dried them, and then went into the right cabinet for the pan. He placed a few of the squares onto the pan and then put it in the oven. He set the timer for fifteen minutes, and then he and I went over to the family room and loved on little Gianna. She was a happy baby, giving us tons of smiles and baby sounds, and we enjoyed her. When the timer went off, Royal got up and hurried to the kitchen, pulling the pan from the oven. He grabbed a couple of plates from the cabinet and then sat them on the island. I went over to the family room and put GiGi in her swing. Before he sat, he opened Gabby's wine cooler but then closed the door and went into their pantry.

"Red goes with red sauce," he said and then came out with a bottle of Pinot Noir. He opened it and then poured us both a glass. I was impressed, but not excited because this wasn't a date. We were at his brother and my sister's home, so besides the pizza, we were enjoying their things. "So why do you keep giving me a hard time, Gem, when you know I am feeling you?"

"You charged me for my damn car to be detailed, Royal. Why do you think?"

He chuckled. "Baby, seriously? I know you saw that I refunded yo' shit, so why you still actin' like you are not interested?"

"Because I'm not." I countered.

"I need to know why, though. You are sitting here looking good enough to move my plate of pizza to the fucking side and devour you instead, and I am feeling you, Gem. I mean, your mean ass just fuckin' turns me on, and not to mention I get lost in those damn hazel eyes of yours."

I laughed loudly. "Your joking, right? I mean from the moment we met, all you've given me is attitude and let me add the fact that you and your phone have a special relationship that I can't even begin to compete with."

He laughed again. "I can agree with everything you are saying, love. I won't deny any of it, but your ass ain't the most pleasant ma'fucka to be around at times either, so I give you what you give me. And my phone, have I pulled out my shit since I've walked through the door? No, because I powered that bitch off, and it is in my Infinity because I came to spend time with you and lil GiGi. Anybody that means anything to me knows I am here, and Gutta still got a damn landline. I used to be on my phone so much because I have bitches blowing me up constantly, but I only want one woman now, Gem. I am here because I am seriously interested *in you*. No bullshit, and no games. I like you, Gemma. I mean, I *really* like you."

I stared at him and then blinked a few times. This person, before my eyes, was not the egotistical ass that I had gotten to know. He seemed lovable, caring, and someone that I would consider being with. I opened my mouth, but I was lost for words. I wanted to question him to see if what he said held an ounce of truth, but then my niece began to cry. I turned my attention to her to see what had turned her baby laughter into sobs. "What's wrong, GiGi?" I cooed, and then instantly remember Gutta telling me that she did not like to be wet at all. Even though the diaper manufacturer advertised a dry bottom, he told me that Gianna would go into a fit of cries as soon as piss or shit hit her diaper.

"What's wrong with her?" Royal asked like he was concerned about why she was crying.

"Maybe her diaper. Gabby said her next feeding would be at eight, so I guess she may be a little hungry too."

"No worries, we got this. Point me to the bottles, and you can check her diaper. I will heat up her milk," he offered.

"Since when do you know how to heat up her milk?"

"I watched my big bro. I know it's that bottle with that bag, so a few minutes dipped in hot water should do the trick. Gutta did it a few times in front of me, so I got this," he explained. I gave a point to the fridge where her premade bottles were, and then I took her out of her seat. As soon as her little ass was in the air, I knew it was a number two, but she was my niece, so it didn't bother me one bit to clean her up. I went up to her nursery, strapped her down on her changing table, and then grabbed her wipes, a new diaper, and baby powder. I cleaned her up good, and by the middle of her diaper change, she was all smiles again. I nuzzled her nose with mine and told her how much I adored her before we went back down. As promised, Royal had successfully warmed her bottle to the perfect temperature, and I settled on the sofa to feed her.

Her eyes fluttered as she came close to the last few drops of her milk, and by the time she had sucked out all of the contents, she was asleep. I stood to take her up to her nursery, and Royal was right behind me, so I turned to him. "I don't need help putting her down," I said.

"I know, but I wanted to help put my niece to bed." He seemed to be less asshole and more likable.

I smiled and said. "No, you can clean up this mess, pour me another glass, and let me go up to put her down."

"Easy enough," he returned with that damn lick of his lips that he would do from time to time to make my center quicken, and I rolled my eyes at him before I continued toward the stairs to take GiGi up to her crib. I didn't want to disturb her little sleeping body, but I had to take off her tiny baby jeans, and *I Am My Auntie's Favorite* top. I had found that little top online for her and could not resist getting it. I liked babies, not kids... just babies, but I was sure that GiGi would always be my favorite niece. I got her down without too much of a sleep interruption, and then I headed back down. Royal was on the sectional, and my fresh glass of wine was on the coffee table. I looked at the television, and it was on the Netflix screen, and I couldn't help laughing.

"So, I guess you are infamous for Netflix and chill?" I shot before I flopped down on the sofa next to him.

"No, I am not, but since we are sitting with Gianna, there is not much of anything else we can do in Gutta and Gabby's house, unless you wanna fa—"

He was about to say, but I cut him all the way off. "Umm, nobody wants to fuck, Royal... damn, how can you ruin shit that fast? I was just starting to like ya' ass."

"First of all, Ms. Gemma, I was about to say *foot massage*. You didn't allow me to finish. And if this were all about pussy, I'd be in the damn streets entertaining someone that I know I could easily get the pussy from. I mean maybe, you are hard of fucking hearing or just don't know any damn better, but I have told you that I *like* you, Gemma. Meaning, I respect you, and I am *not* just trying to fuck!" he said and stood. He seemed upset. I didn't mean to make him angry, and I certainly didn't want him to leave.

"Hold, on wait, please... Royal, I apologize. I am sorry, okay." I expressed and stared at him.

"No, Gemma, it's cool. I mean, I am not a thirsty nigga, and there are a million and one places that I could be right now."

I trembled a bit because I knew that was a fact. "I know Royal, and again, I am sorry, okay. I mean, you being this attentive and this guy that you are being right now is new to me because since the night I met you, you've been in asshole mode, so please, sit. I don't want you to leave."

He sighed, ran a hand over his head, down his face, and over his beard. He eased back down onto the sofa with me, and I smiled. "If I weren't feeling yo' lil mean ass, I'd be out. I mean, yo' ass gotta always be fucking difficult," he said and relaxed onto the cushion.

I moved closer to him and rested under his arm. "Well, what you see is what the fuck you get. I'm not in the pretending business. I am who I am."

"I know, and I like it. I like you for you, but understand, I have options baby, so you need to act like you got some fucking sense."

I clicked my tongue. "Boy, whatever!" I said and snatched up the remote. We went back and forth, trying to select a movie; and finally, we just decided to listen to some music. We talked and sipped, and by three, the sounds of my niece's cries came through the baby monitor, alerting me that my niece was ready for another meal. I went up for her while Royal warmed her bottle again. We both doted over little GiGi while she ate and played with her with funny sounds and baby talk. By five, she was back to sleep, and we both cuddled on the family room sectional as we got a few winks. By nine, GiGi was up again. I got a taste of what my sister had been going through with her baby, and I didn't want any of that shit. By one, Royal and I were laughing and enjoying each other when our siblings walked in. We were in the family room, entertaining our adorable niece again when they walked in.

Gabby came over to pick up Gianna like she had been away at war for a year, and Gutta was right by her side as if they hadn't seen GiGi in years. I looked at Royal, and we both agreed that it was time to leave. We bid our farewells to the married couple and their offspring and headed to our cars. "So, do you wanna hang, or do you have other plans?" Royal asked.

"No plans, but since I switched up my schedule, I have a double shift tomorrow, so I really should be getting home."

"But I'm not tired of your mean ass yet. I can come over, keep you company."

I smiled. "Fine, give me your phone," I said.

"And why do you want my phone?"

"Ain't nobody trying to look through yo' shit or scope out all of your ho's. I just want to put my number in your phone."

"Aw'ight, I am good with that... hold on, let me get it."

He walked over to his vehicle and got his phone. I watched him press the button to power it on as he walked in my direction. After he keyed in his code, he handed his iPhone over to me. I didn't bother trying to snoop. I just went straight to his contacts and added myself. I then hit the call button, and when my phone sang my ringtone in my purse, I hit end and then gave it back to him. "I will text you my address, in case you get lost on the way."

"You do that, sexy," he said with that sensual, devilish grin that not only drove me crazy but resembled his big brother Malice. Malice gave that same little grin to my sister, and I shook my damn head. He opened my door, and I got in, and I waited for him to get into his SUV before I pulled away. I didn't know what the fuck was going on, but I was suddenly falling for his ass. "Fuck, fuck, fuck, fuck, fuuucccccck-kkkkk!" I spat after I pulled away.

✨ 4 ✨

ROYAL

My phone alerted me with a text, and it was her address. I quickly went to my info settings to save her number before I pulled away. I keyed in *Gemma*, then I backspaced that shit and put in *Mean Ass*. I clicked add photo and went to my pictures and saved one of the pics that I took at the reception of her smiling with her sisters. It was a beautifully captured moment of her, and she looked stunning in that pic. I admired it for a second or two and then cranked my engine. It was a bit brisk, and I should have started my vehicle as soon as I got in, but Miss Mean Ass warmed my insides, so I pretty much ignored the elements. I sent her a quick text back, saying I got it and asked if she wanted me to grab her something because I was a bit hungry.

Mean Ass – YES, WHATEVER YOU GET ME IS COOL, I'M NOT PICKY

Me – COOL, I GOT U BABE

With that, I watched her pull out of the circular cobblestone drive-way. I decided to run by my place first to shower and change since she didn't live too far from me. I had never known that we lived in the same area, but I figured since she worked at Mercy, she'd be at a reasonable distance from her job. When I made it to my townhouse, I hurried inside. After I showered, changed, and smelled like Bond 9, I texted her.

Me – GONNA ORDER FRM 14 PARISH, HAV U EATEN THERE B4?

Mean Ass – SOUNDS GOOD & YES I HAVE. THAT COCONUT CURRY SHRIMP BE HITTIN'

Me – COOL, I WILL B THERE SOON

Mean Ass – CAN YOU GET ME A PINEAPPLE SODA PLS

Me – I GOT U

I called in our order and headed out. I picked up our food, and when I made it to her place, I had to find a parking space on the street. The one thing I hated about my SUV, it was hard as hell to find a space large enough at times, especially when you wanted to park close. I found something a little way up her block, then I hiked it back to her building. I rung her bell, and she buzzed me in. I ran up the three flights of steps that seemed like four, and she was standing in the doorway, waiting. I smiled. "Hey there," I said, coming up the last few steps.

"Hey," she returned with a cute little smirk.

I quickly leaned in for a kiss. She let my lips cover hers, and then we went inside. Her space was bright with all of her curtains opened, and it looked like I'd expected. Cozy with warm shades of brown, beige, burgundy, and tan with a few black accents. Very neutral and a nice warm feeling. I could see she had dark hardwoods, but she had a sizeable beige rug, large enough to go under her furniture. I noticed she had a lot of plants and charming décor adorning her walls, and the aroma of something floral was dancing in the air. I handed her the packages of food and then removed my jacket.

"The coat closet is there," she said, giving a point as she headed to the kitchen, I assumed, walking towards what looked like a dining room. I hung my coat and headed into that direction, and as I figured, she was in her kitchen. It also gave a warm feeling with dark cabinets, light browns, gold, and a speckle of black in her glass backsplash and all stainless-steel appliances. The floor was also the same hardwoods that carried out throughout the house. The packages were on the counter, and I watched her pull plates from the cabinet. "Did you want to eat here in the kitchen or in the dining room?" she asked.

"All up to you, either is good for me."

"Here is fine, and you can have a seat. I got this," she said.

"Can you point me to your bathroom? I'd like to wash my hands," I requested.

"Sure, it's on the other side in the hall near the bedrooms, you can't miss it."

I walked through the dining room, and right when I entered the living room, a hall was on my right. I turned, and the bathroom was directly in front of me. I went in to see that her bathroom was just as lovely and clean as the rest of her place and the dark rustic gold, black with a hint of gray slate tiles were on the floor and on the walls of her entire shower. It looked beautiful, and I was comfortable at Gemma's place. I washed my hands and used the hand towel that was on the vanity to dry my hands. I made my way back to the kitchen, and she was putting the plates of food onto the table. Since Gemma knew what she wanted, I was sure she realized the jerk catfish was mine. I had also ordered some crab cakes, and I was ready to dig in, so I sat. "Your place is really nice, babe. It definitely looks like your style."

"Thanks. Gracie did most of the decorating because I had no clue what I wanted my place to look like. I didn't move out of Gloria Jean's house until I was ready to buy, so we spent four weeks painting and doing little projects to make it cute prior to me moving in. The slate tile was already here, but no vanity, only a pedestal sink, and there was no color on the walls and no backsplash in my kitchen. The appliances were mixed matched, and the light fixtures and ceiling fans were outdated. Gracie is such a DIY fanatic, she would come over every single day after court and every single weekend to glam it up. She made the vanity in my bathroom out of an old cabinet that she refurbished. She and I changed out all the light fixtures, ceiling fans, and we put in that beautiful backsplash along with my daddy for all of the heavy lifting. I was terrified to do any of it on my own, but Gracie would sit me down and show me all of these YouTube tutorials on how to do shit myself."

"When I first got my place, money was super tight, but Gracie helped me find my living room set for only one hundred bucks."

"No fucking way! Not the furniture that is in your living room?" I questioned.

"Yes, way, and then we hit up Hobby Lobby, found the perfect fabric on clearance I must add, and my beautiful sofa and loveseat cost me less than four hundred dollars."

"Damn, yo' sis reupholstered your furniture to make it look that nice?"

"She did, and my closets are perfectly organized down to my belts because of my big sis."

"Damn, Grace got skills. She should be working with Rel," I said and then took a bite of my food.

"She does, and you should see her artwork. She has been sketching and drawing since we were kids, and she is the one that God gave a ton of creative talent too because she does almost everything, you hear me? She is a better cook than Gabby and I. She is the only sister that knows how to not only change a tire, but she can keep up the maintenance on a vehicle... no lie because she spent way more time with Gloria Jean in the kitchen and Boris at his shop than Gab and me. And when she sings, Royal... when she sings, my sister *sangs*. I mean, my mom and I can sing too, but Gracie, oh my God... her voice is so powerful and strong that it likes moves your spirit and touches your insides," she expressed, making a serious face with her eyes closed and her right hand over her heart. She took a deep breath before opening her eyes and picking up her fork. Gemma took a huge bite of her food, moaning as she chewed. Her moans sounded like she may have had some pipes, but I'd have to hear her voice to confirm what I thought would be the voice of an angel.

"So, you sing too?" I quickly jumped in.

She chewed and swallowed. "Yes, I do. Not my favorite thing to do, but yes, God blessed me with vocal talent."

"Okay, then show me what you got."

"Umm, no. I am eating and not in a singing mood," she said and shoveled more rice and shrimp into her mouth.

"I don't usually beg a woman for a damn thing, but I am so curious to know what you sound like singing versus talking a whole lot of shit."

"Ha, ha, ha, Kevin Hart, but no. I have to be in the right mood to sing, and right now, I am hungry and want to eat all of this deliciousness off of my plate."

"Okay, I will let you slide this time, but I wanna see what you got, Ms. Gemma."

She playfully rolled her eyes. "Whatever Mr. Royal," she said, and we continued small talk as we finished our meals. I stayed and kept her company while she loaded the dishwasher with the couple of dishes that we used. Before going to the sofa, she fixed me a Henny and Coke and then poured herself a glass of white. We shared a few drinks and talked about everything and then nothing at all. By ten, she was yawning, and since the next day was Sunday for me, I didn't want to leave.

"You sleepy, baby?" I asked, knowing that she was. Her beautiful face was radiant and make-up free, but I knew the look of exhaustion.

"I am, and I so wish that I didn't have to do a double tomorrow, but hey, I should have done my 7-3 yesterday," she said, yawning.

I stood. "I can go, babe, so you can get some rest."

She stood. "Yes, it is time for me to lay it down."

I nodded and headed toward the closet to get my coat, and she was right behind me. I wished she wanted me to stay, but I wasn't about to come off as too fucking thirsty, so I declined on asking her if I could stay. I pulled my jacket from the hanger and put it on. She kept her eyes locked on me, and I kept my eyes locked on her. When I leaned in to kiss her, she allowed my tongue to playfully dance with hers. I didn't want to stop because she just tasted so damn good. I grabbed her ass, and when she held onto my jacket, my damn dick stiffened, causing me to pull back. "I should go," I said.

"I know, but I honestly don't want you too."

"I can stay, Gem. I mean, I don't have shit going on tomorrow. I can even take you to work and pick you up," I offered. For some reason, I wanted to do anything I could to make shit easy for her if she allowed me to stay.

"I'd like that, and I have a Roku in my bedroom that has headphones in case you want to watch something. I just have to sleep so I can be fully alert tomorrow."

"That's cool," I said before removing my jacket. I hung it back into her closet and followed her to her room. It was a lot bigger than I imagined it would be, and she had a king-sized bed. I figured we could both rest easy without me disturbing her too much. She got me set up with the Roku remote and then got into the bed. She had an oversized chair and ottoman, so I decided to sit in it while I watched television and played around on my phone. "Babe," I called out.

"Yeah," she answered softly.

"I know that that's maybe your favorite side of the bed and whatnot, but a man should always sleep near the door."

"Is that right?" she asked.

"That is what my pops always taught my brothers and me growing up," I said.

She smiled, but then slowly moved over to the other side of the bed. "Well, my piece is in that top drawer," she said, pointing at the nightstand on the side of the bed that she was vacating as she slid over to the other side.

"You strapped?" I quizzed.

"I am. Momma doesn't know, but since I am the baby, daddy gave me a little pink and silver 38 special and taught me how to use it when I first moved out on my own."

"Fun facts about my future wife and baby momma," I joked.

"What the hell eva, Royal," she said as she made herself comfortable on the other side of the bed. She turned her back, and I turned my attention back to the television. I stayed awake for a couple of hours after she went to sleep and watched a movie on Netflix. It wasn't late for me on a Saturday night, and a huge part of me wanted to go to Desire or Passion's for a drink and a night of fun, but the more substantial part of me wanted to get in bed and wake her with my dick in hand. I wanted to taste her pussy and see what she was working with between them thick ass thighs of hers, but I knew that she wasn't that easy.

I was totally good with waiting and taking things slow with Gemma, but I was still a man and wanted to experience her heat. I knew some women held out, and if that was what Gemma was on, I'd be cool with that, but I had to admit I wanted all of her. The bad attitude, smart ass mouth, brilliant ass nurse, outgoing spirit, and bottom-line gorgeousness that she owned. When she walked in, my ego would double up, and I was always on one-hunnit to match clever wits and smart remarks with her. Her attitude was what turned me on, and verbally sparring with her made shit just interesting, but now, I needed to tap into the side of her that was romantic, girly, and sweet. I knew that if I played my romantic cards right, I could disengage her fierce demeanor and make her all mine. I mean, I didn't want to change her because I loved the battlefield that she and I played on, but I wanted to break her down where we could spar and also love on each other just as hard.

After the movie that I had watched, I removed the headphones and then my clothes down to my boxers. It was after eleven, and I knew she had to be at work by seven, so I set my alarm for five a.m. I climbed into bed, and she didn't reject my body as I cuddled close to her. I kissed the back of her neck and whispered goodnight into her ear softly, and she didn't even stir. I closed my eyes and begged my dick to not swell as I laid next to her soft skin, but it had a mind of its own. I coached myself not to be that lame ass nigga, who mannishly touched her body while she slept, and rested my hand on her thigh. I closed my eyes and thought of all things other than the fat, wet pussy, and the plump ass that rested against my dick and mid-section. I touched her tenderly and rested my hand on her smooth rounded hip, and told my dick to calm down. I eventually fell into a deep sleep, not sure if it was before or after my big dick deflated.

❧ 5 ❧

CHAS

My eyes fluttered as I struggled to open them. I was awoken from my nap by the aroma of something fabulous, but my eyelids weren't in line with my stomach; if they were, it would have been no struggle to open them. Once they were wide opened and I looked around, my eyes landed on my new husband and a man in uniform, moving the dishes from the wheeled cart onto the dining table that was in our open suite. It was day two of our honeymoon in Aruba because day one of the night of our wedding was spent downtown in a fancy honeymoon suite. Our tickets were scheduled for later that night, and so damn early the next morning that we didn't sleep. We left the reception, went to our room, stripped out of our clothes, and made love. We then showered together, dressed, and headed to the airport.

There was no sleep on our wedding night, but as soon as we were airborne and exchanged a kiss, my new husband and I fell into a deep, coma-like sleep. The flight attendant had to shake us to wake us, but I wasn't mad because my husband and I got off the plane fully rested and ready to enjoy our honeymoon. Everything was so beautiful and first-class. My husband had done a fantastic job with planning everything on his own. We were not billionaires, but the entire experience had me feeling like we were. There was no way the smile on my face could be removed. There was nothing that I'd want to be better or different, and I knew my husband, and I would enjoy our seven-day getaway.

Once we were in our beachfront villa, I *ooohed* and *aahed* at everything. "Oh my God, Rel, baby, this cannot be ours?" I said, smiling like a Cheshire cat.

"It is ours, babe, and please don't think that I held out on you when I told you how much my company was worth. Remember my client Mr. Patel, the first hotel that my company built?"

"Yes babe, that is like your success story, how could I forget?"

He nodded because he knew that I had heard that story tons of times. "Well, when he got our wedding invitation, he suggested that we honeymoon here. This is his brother's place, and we are staying here in all of this gloriousness for close to nothing," he said.

"Shut the front door!" I said. I knew that piece of heaven may have set us back a decade if we were paying full price for it. I mean, it was just that glorious, and it was like the beach was our backyard.

"Baby, I am so serious. You are going to love this place, and we are going to have the best honeymoon," he said, moving in close to me. He wrapped his arms around me and nuzzled my neck and planted a few soft kisses on my collar bone. "We are going to eat good, enjoy a few adventures, and make love so many times that we lose count."

"Now, don't be making no promises that your dick can't keep, baby," I said, jokingly, and my husband turned me to face him.

"Baby, my dick is here to please you anytime, any moment, and any which way you like. My dick is waiting on your command to do whatever you desire it to do."

"Really, now?" I said, undoing the buttons on his shirt. I kissed my husband down his chest and then went into a squat, going straight for my husband's rod. As soon as it was freed from his boxers and linen pants, I pulled his head and entire shaft into my mouth. I sucked him eagerly as his pole grew larger in my mouth. I more than enjoyed my husband's scent and the fresh, clean taste of his soft skin. I loved Rel's chest, stomach, shoulders, and arms, but his dick was my fucking favorite. Whether it was in my mouth or in my core, it pleased me, and with that, I always aimed to please him. I loved that my body made him feel good, allowing Rel to fuck my mouth smooth, easy, and the shots that hit my throat didn't make me gag. The sounds of his growls and groans were the accent of how he sometimes pulled my hair.

I sucked, bobbed, lick, and spit on his nightstick as he held my head, pushing his head to the depths of my throat. When his semen exploded and flooded my mouth, I swallowed but allowed some to drip down the side of my mouth for visuals. He loved to see me lick his cream no matter where it landed, and I had no problem giving my husband bad girl behavior because he loved that shit. It was our honeymoon, and I was so in love with Rel, whatever he asked for that week, I'd give it to him. After I licked all traces of his creamy goodness, he began to pull away my dress and rolled my thongs down, leaving my things right on the tiled patio floor. He grabbed me by the hand, and I followed him over to the infinity pool. We got in and played around for a little while. I wrapped my legs around his waist and my arms around his neck and rode him so easy with the motion of the water. When I exploded, I called out Rel's name ten times as my thighs trembled. We got out of the water, went for the outdoor shower, and made love again on the oversized heart-shaped lawn furniture. We drank champagne, and after he licked me to another orgasm, I climbed into the bed and took a long nap. Now I was awake and ready to dig into whatever they were setting up at the table. I waited till the concierge vacated the room before I threw the covers back from my naked body.

I stood and walked over to my man, wrapping my arms around him from the back. "I was just about to wake you, babe," he said.

"Man, you know my nose woke me with that marvelous aroma of food. What'd you order for us?"

"Lobster tails, king crab legs, and shrimp scampi, of course."

I held him even tighter. "All of my favorites, babe," I said and kissed his back. He was shirtless, and his skin felt so damn good against my face.

"Indeed, and a couple of salads and baked potatoes."

"Let me go and freshen up, and I'll be right back." I hurried to the bathroom and just rinsed my mouth with water. I didn't want the taste of toothpaste to ruin my meal. I washed my face and wet my hair down again, brushing it back into a ponytail. I glossed my lips and put on a see-through lace dress that hugged my everything. It was not lingerie, but it was inside wear for your man's eyes only, and it was perfect for our intimate dinner. I hit my right spots with my Very Sexy body spray and went back to join my husband at the table.

"Damn, Chas, I am debating should I be eating *you* or this damn food in front of me," he said.

I smiled and then grabbed the wine to fill our glasses. "Eat your dinner, baby, and you can have me for dessert after," I teased.

"I will, baby... that is for damn sure," he said. We ate, and I just gazed at him. It was like I had no memories of the hellish marriage I had experienced with Chris; it was now like a damn blur. I was just so happy at that moment and hoped that I'd be able to give Rel children. Chris and I conceived once, but he had beaten me so bad one time during that pregnancy, I had lost the baby. After that, I never got pregnant again. The hell that I went through with Chris had me grateful we hadn't had a child together, but until Rel came along, not being able to have babies was never in the forefront of my mind. Rel and I talked about kids and how we both wanted at least two, but we hadn't set a timeline for anything. Now that we were married, I was sure that subject would come up again. I was terrified that that would be the only thing that I couldn't give him.

"What's going on in that pretty little head of yours?" he asked, interrupting my thoughts. I hadn't realized that I had gotten so quiet. We had finished dinner and took a walk on the beach and played around in the water for a little while. I wanted to leave our room to see what else Aruba had to offer, but he assured me that he had so many things planned for us that week. He wanted us to just stay in and make love our first night there. I agreed, and we were relaxing on the hammock together.

"Nothing babe, just lying here thinking how perfect things are right now. Yesterday, marrying you was the happiest day of my entire life. I know this is my second marriage, but I didn't feel half as good as I felt yesterday when I exchanged vows with you. I mean, I felt a different kind of energy. Bae, I can't explain it, Rel. Like if this is what real and true love feels like, I didn't love Chris. And if I did, it was certainly not this deeply."

"I can understand bae. I mean, I have cared deeply, even liked a woman a great deal, but no woman has ever made me feel like this. To simply put it, it's like my love for you makes me fearless... like I'd risk everything, even my life, to make you happy, Chas. I know we've had this conversation before, but if Malice hadn't laid Chris to rest, I may have ended up killing him myself for just putting his muthafuckin' hands on you. That night, all I could do was see your face. I know if my brothers hadn't shown up when they did, and he had pulled that gun out, I would have died that night because I would have dived on that nigga to save you."

I looked up at my husband. "I know, babe, and I am so glad that things went the way they did because if you had died that night protecting me Rel, I'd be a basket case."

He squeezed me tighter. "I know, and I am glad Malice put two in his chest for all the hell and the bullshit he put you through... eventually, I would have sent his ass to the morgue if he wouldn't have backed the fuck up."

"I guess you Wilkerson men fight to the death for the ones you love?" I asked. I wanted to ask him about Gutta and Trina. He was my husband now, and I knew Gabby lied through her damn teeth about Gutta killing that bitch. I wasn't even mad that she lied and defended her husband because if shit had been reversed and Rel had killed Chris, I'd never admit it to a soul either, not even my best friend, so I knew why Gabby didn't tell me the real.

"We do, babe. I mean that none of this shit was planned. I was hoping Chris would have stayed away. I am sure Malice didn't expect Silk's ass to come at Grace, even though technically Malice didn't kill him... that street business caught up with him, but for Grace... I know that Malice would have killed his bitch ass with no hesitation."

"And Trina?" I asked my husband.

"Let's just say, she didn't know how to sit her ass down, so she learned the hard way babe. We are not thugs or street kings or no shit like that, but we boss up when we have to, and just like I'd die for you, Chas, I'd kill for you if provoked."

I rested my head on my husband's chest. "I'd do the same for you, baby... no question. Shit has been crazy, and I am glad all of that madness is behind us."

He kissed the top of my head and just held me even tighter. "So am I, and I hope baby Royal and Miss Gemma have better luck than we all had. I mean, it has been a lot of damn drama with us all," he chuckled.

"I think they are good. All the bad guys and gals are gone, so it's our time to just live our best lives. Gemma plays the role like she doesn't like Royal, but her ass ain't fooling nobody."

"Well, I know my baby bro got it bad for her ass because I've never seen that fool act like he got some damn sense. Now when he is around her, he is on good behavior," he laughed lightly.

"All I can say to that is the right woman will change a man."

"I agree one thousand percent because, before yo' ass, there were never any damn sleepovers at my house, but this peach you got between them thighs baby got me fucking hooked."

"And I planned to keep you hooked on this," I said and moved to get on top of him. I kissed him deeply and passionately while his hands roamed my ass; and before long, we were doing new tricks in that damn hammock. I was in love and happy that Rel was my man.

❧ 6 ☙

GEMMA

As promised, Royal was waiting for me when I walked out of the hospital doors. I had had a long ass day, and I was so ready to get outta my scrubs and wash the stench of the hospital off of my skin. He got out when he saw me approach his Infinity, opened the door for me, and helped me climb in. He shut my door and went around and got back in the driver's seat.

"Thanks," I said as soon as he shut his door.

"Thanks for what, babe?"

"For picking me up. I am dog tired, you hear me?"

"I can imagine, being here for sixteen hours ain't no damn joke, and I missed you today."

I blushed. "Did you?"

"I did, and I took the liberty of bringing you a plate from my mom's, and when we get to your place, I will gladly give you a foot rub and a glass of Chardonnay."

"I am starving too. And don't you start no shit that you can't keep up Mr. Royal because how you get me is what you will be expected to do to keep me."

"Copy that," he said, leaning over the seat for a kiss, and I gave him a quick peck. He put his truck in gear, and we headed towards my place. I would never tell his ass, but every brief moment I had that day when I wasn't busy, I thought of him too and could not wait to see him. He kept invading my thoughts when I tried not to even think of him, and a smile crept on my lips every time I thought about him.

"So, do you work tomorrow?" I asked him.

"I do. I normally work Monday through Saturday, but since the wedding went down on Friday, I took the entire weekend off."

"Okay, so I can bring my Audi to your shop tomorrow after I get off work?" I asked with a smirk.

"I got a better one for you, boo. I'll come by and pick it up for you, have it detailed, and then bring it back before your shift is done."

"Yeah, okay... for how much? I mean, last I heard, you said we have to work out a deal in order for me to get my car detailed for free."

"Well that was then, now it's different. Plus, you act like I didn't refund your damn money. I only swiped yo' shit because yo' damn mouth is so smart."

"You keep actin' like an ass, and you will never see what else this smart-ass mouth can do," I snapped back.

He grabbed his dick. "Damn Gem, baby, it's like that?"

"It is. I mean, as soon as we good, here yo' ass go talking about my mouth being smart and shit, and I haven't cussed yo' ass out since before the wedding. However, if you want me to give you this smart-ass mouth, go ahead, start talkin' shit, boo... you know I'm ready to check dat ass," I said playfully. I loved going toe to toe with him, and as tired as I was, I was never too tired to go a round with Royal's ass.

"Damn, bae, bring all that shit down, aw'ight. I got you, ma... I will take care of yo' ride baby, damn. We good on that, and if you can show me what else that mouth can do tonight, I'm wit it," he added.

I playfully rolled my eyes at him. "You wish," I said with a smirk. "Let me see how nice my ride looks tomorrow, and then I may tip yo' ass wit a lil sumthin' sumthin,'" I flirted.

"Well, that shit is easy because my shop on-point wit' it and tomorrow, yo' baby gon' be restored back to brand new when I get done wit' it, for real, for real."

"We shall see," I said and sucked my teeth. I was hating that I was feeling Royal's pain in the ass, ass. He was just creeping into my heart, and I was feeling way more attracted to him than I wanted to be. I mean, I wanted to do more than just kiss him. I wanted to see what he could do with those sexy ass lips, and damn sure wanted to know if he was slinging dick like Gabby, Chas, and Gracie described when we talked about Gutta, Rel, and Malice. If he had inherited the Wilkerson bedroom skills, I might be his next number one.

7

GABBY

I put my bundle down and hurried to my phone. I smiled when I saw my bestie Chas' name on my screen. I answered by the fourth ring. "Good afternoon, Mrs. Wilkerson," I said with a huge smile on my face. It had been a week and three days since my best friend had tied the knot, and I was dying to hear the details of her and Rel's honeymoon.

"Well, good afternoon to you too, Mrs. Wilkerson," she returned, and I could hear the smile in her voice.

"I am so happy to hear your voice, girl. I mean, I didn't know that I'd miss your ass while you were away."

"Well, if you and Gutta had paused and honeymooned out of Chicago, I'd say I know what you felt, but you were pregnant, and y'all only had a weekend away."

"Yes, but it was all rush, rush, and no real-time to plan the perfect honeymoon like you and Rel, so give me all of the juicy details."

"Oh, my Lord, Gabby, it was like the best time of my life. We got out, did a few things like tours, dinner, horseback riding, massages, and a lot of water things, but girl, I must tell you that the lovemaking was out of this fucking world. My husband and I fucked in every position you can dream of. Feast on each other's organs like we could digest each other, and there were moments when our skin slapped so damn loud against each other that I knew the entire island had to hear us—had me on a level of happiness that no words can describe Gabby. I mean, I think I fell even deeper in love with Rel in the last ten days since I said I do. Who knew love could be this damn good? We still have a couple of days before we return to work, but Gabby, I am literally addicted to this man and don't know if I am ready to spend a second without him or a minute without him inside of me. I mean, just the way he kisses me."

"Damn, Chas, I thought Gutta and I were explosive. You make me wanna hang-up and go jump on my husband's dick right now," I said, playfully fanning my face.

"And you should. The only reason I am not all over Rel at this very minute is that we needed food up in this damn house girl. We cleaned mostly everything out before the wedding, so nothing would spoil while we were away, and since we've been back, we've been ordering in. Now you know Rel is health-conscious and not big on take-out, so he agreed to shop, and hell, my spoil ass didn't argue."

"I know that is real. One thing I can give Gutta so much credit for is that he takes care of whatever needs to be taken care of with no fuss. He caters to lil GiGi and me like we are a princess and queen. I can honestly say that our sex life is not as hot as it was before the baby, but I am working my way back to that. I be so tired at times, Chas, and even though Gutta doesn't say it, I know he misses what we were like before the baby."

"I can only imagine Gab, and that is what actually prompted my call," she said.

Confused, I asked, "How is *my* sex life with Gutta a reason for your call? Did he say something to Rel? I mean, I know they are close, but how could he go to Rel and not me?" I huffed.

"No, Gab, baby, please calm down. Your husband hasn't gone to my husband as far as I know about y'all sex or bedroom woes. Even if he did, I am sure Rel would never break any bro codes. I am talking about kids, Gab. I am calling you because, on our honeymoon, Rel expressed how he wanted to start a family right away, but I am terrified that I can't."

"Can't what, Chas, give him children? I mean, come on, you knew this before you two got married. And you can't go the selfish route on this, Chas... you will be a great mother."

"No, no, Gab, that's not it. I am afraid that I *can't* have children," she said.

I heard her but found that so hard to believe. "Chas, no way are you infertile. I mean, why would you get an IUD if you can't have babies?"

"I got it just so I wouldn't get pregnant by a random dude, Gabby. I had it removed two weeks before the wedding. My doctor did explain that it may take a few months, but I think Chris fucked up something down there, Gab. You were in Texas when I had that miscarriage after he beat the dog shit out of me. No doctor has ever just said, "no, I can't have kids," but I am so afraid that I can't," she sniffled into the phone.

I paused and took a deep breath so I could give my friend the soundest advice that I could. "Listen, baby, God is good. He delivered you from Chris and gave you your ten-fold with Rel. No matter how you and your husband can and will be parents. Even if your womb can't carry a child Chas, we will figure it all out, just enjoy your husband and make love to him over and over again. Give it six months, and if in six months we are not pregnant, then we seek medical attention. Our God is in control, do you hear me? And we don't have a say. Just pray, believe, and trust him. Infertility doesn't mean you can't mother a child," I said gently.

She sniffled. "You are so right, my friend. That is why I called you. You always know the right things to say."

"I try. I am not the most perfect person, but I believe in a higher power, and I repent and strive for excellence," I said.

"Ain't that so true," my best friend said into the phone. At that moment, I felt a need to tell my best friend the truth about Trina, but my doorbell chimed. Gutta was downstairs, but I headed towards the stairs to see who was at our door.

"Hold on bestie," I said when I saw my door was opened to two uniformed officers. "Chas, baby, I need to call you back," I said and then ended the call. I hurried down the steps to see why they were at our doorstep.

"Am I under arrest?" My husband questioned.

"No, sir, you are not, but we need you to come down to the station with us so we can ask you some questions."

"If there are only questions, why does my husband have to go down to the station?" I shot.

"It's just routine ma'am, no one's under arrest," the officer assured me, but still, that shit wasn't settling right with me.

"If he is not under arrest, my husband doesn't have to go anywhere," I refuted.

"Baby, it's okay. I have nothing to hide, so no worries."

He said it so smoothly and calmly, but I was worried. I didn't know what they knew, and I did not want my husband to go to jail for murdering a stalking bitch named Trina. "Are you sure baby?" I asked, looking him in the eyes. My question was innocent enough to the cops, but I was asking him was he one thousand percent sure that he was in the clear.

He nodded. "Baby, on my life, I can assure you that everything is good. You have nothing to worry about, Muffy," he said with a smile. He gave me a soft kiss on my lips and then pulled me in close to him. "We are good," he whispered in my ear and then kissed my cheek. I trusted my husband, so I nodded and exhaled. Not long after I got the news of Trina's murder, Gutta sat me down and explained how Bash was like a brother to him and would never allow shit to come back to him. Gutta assured me that he would never be implemented for Trina's murder. And even though his trip to the station had me shook, I believed my husband, and I fully trusted my man, but I needed my girls. As soon as I shut the door, I sobbed and tried to hold it together on my own, but after three hours, I texted Grace first. I don't know why I reached out to Grace first, but that was who I text. Within minutes, Grace called and said she and Malice were on their way. She convinced me to call Gemma and assured me that telling Chas and Tori would be okay. Not long after the call, they were all in my family room. I told them all the truth about what was going on, and they all somehow already knew that it was a strong possibility, but no one would ever share that with one outside of that room. I believed my family and trusted them because I knew they all knew the trouble that Trina had caused for our lives.

We mostly sat in silence until my phone finally rang. It was Gutta, and he was free to go. The men insisted they go and get him while we stayed at my house with the baby, and I thought that would be best. We all talked about the subject of Trina, and they all just kept reassuring me that all would be okay. I was so grateful to have the support of my family and close friends.

"Rel would have done the same for me and Malice would have done the exact same for Grace, and the rate Gemma is going, Royal for her. We have a family of no-nonsense men on our hands, and they just handle shit. Trina was a problem Gab and Gutta did what Rel and Malice would have done to keep his own safe. They are boss men, getting up every day taking care of business and us, so I am not mad that you didn't tell me, Gabby. Deep down inside, I already knew," Chas said to me.

"I am so sorry for lying to you, Chas, but now that you are married, you know that there are some things that are just between you and your husband," I said.

"I know," she agreed. A few moments later, my husband walked in with his brothers. Everyone moved quickly to their ladies, and when I saw Royal hug my baby sis from behind, I knew I'd have to get up to speed on what was going on with them. I had been in *mommy mode* and wasn't socializing as much. Gutter explained that they figured out that Trina had been shot somewhere else and then put in her car. Her best friend, Jasmine, said that he was the only one that had it in for her. They questioned my husband for six long hours, basically trying to make him confess to something or slip up by changing his story; but since they didn't have shit on him, it went around in circles with them thinking their threats to close his clubs and taking away our daughter would persuade him to give them anything, but it didn't work. Gutta was a brilliant man, and when he walked through the door with his brothers, I felt a sense of relief and joy. What my husband had done was a crime in the public eye, but for me, he had done justice. When a person comes for you and the ones you love, they take a chance on getting dealt with. In Trina's situation, it was extreme but so fucking necessary, and I still admired my man for protecting what was his. Trina was now an afterthought, and all that matter was Gutter, GiGi, and me.

❧ 8 ❧

GRACE

I sat in the courtroom after a couple of weeks of being off, and my hand shook as I tried to sketch the man sitting in the hot seat. There were like four counts against him for something that I had decided not to digest. Every time he looked my way, I froze like a paranoid idiot. I couldn't shake the feeling of uneasiness being in that courtroom. I wasn't a key witness, nor would I have any reason to testify against him, but I feared that he'd want to come after me for just drawing his face. I tried to keep it together, but I could not. And I was two seconds from damn near having a full-blown attack and involuntarily stood out of my chair. "Your honor, I am so sorry, and I know I am out of order, but can we please have a brief recess?" I requested. I had sat in enough court cases to know what to say.

"Are you okay, Miss Jackson?" she questioned with irritancies.

"No, ma'am, I am not. I just need a few moments, please," I said as my head dropped, but I quickly lifted it to look her in the eyes. Malice had been coaching me on keeping my head up and not allowing shit to go down that made me unhappy, uncomfortable, or upset. I was learning how to be a stronger me. I knew that the man that was on the stand may not have any intentions on my life, but the fear that I was feeling told me that my days in court would be a thing of the past. What was next for me was the big question.

"The court will take a twenty-minute recess, and Ms. Jackson, please meet me in my chambers," she said, and I nodded. I gathered my things, tossed them into my satchel, and made my way to the judge's chambers. I tapped on her door. "Come on in," I heard her say. I walked in slowly and tried to gather words that I wanted to say to her, but they were stuck in my throat. "Do you want to tell me why you put a pause on my case when the man accused is failing miserably to convince the jury that he is innocent?"

"Your honor, I do apologize, and I don't take any of this lightly or as a joke. But since the attempt on my life by a man that I put behind bars, I don't think I want to do this job anymore."

"Grace, you are sweet, but I am not the one you need to be telling this to. I mean, I like you. You are a phenomenal artist and human being, but you are assigned to my cases, not the other way around. And after you leave, they will easily replace you. So just finish out the day, and then you fly the coupe, start over, or whatever you young folks say today, but please, if you change your mind, don't interrupt my proceedings again," she said and stood. "Oh, but to be real, I am glad you did when you did. I had chili dogs, and the bathroom is screaming my name, please let yourself out." She headed to the bathroom, and I headed out the door. I finished out my day and then got with my immediate supervisor and gave my two weeks' notice. Still unsure what would be next, I had to talk to Malice. I had just quick my job with no plan B. I got off the elevator and was pleased to smell the scent of dinner. "Hey, babe," I said as I took off my coat, boots, and scarf, hanging my things before joining him. I was all moved in and could not wait until Rel started on my art room and she space. Malice's place was perfect for us, and going home to him and Bistro every night was the only thing that I looked forward to nowadays.

"Hey, baby," he said to me as I hung my coat. "How was your day, Princess?"

I walked over to the island and took a seat first before I quickly blurted, "I quit my job."

"Okayyyyyyy," he dragged out. "Why? I thought you loved your job."

"I did, I mean... I used too, or maybe I still do, Malice. I am paranoid like all the time now, baby, and I just can't draw the faces of criminals anymore," I declared. The things that went down with Silky still had me shook, and I didn't realize that it had such a significant effect on me.

"Okay, baby, that is fine, but you love your job... and you can't let what went down with Silky destroy your passion. You told me over and over again how much you love what you do, so please don't let fear drive you from a job you love. Silky is dead and gone, so we keep living our best lives," my man said before placing a plate of goodness in front of me. The aroma was insane, and I was ready to eat. I slid off the stool and went over to the sink and washed my hands. What Malice said was so right, but I was not feeling the courtroom anymore. I didn't want another criminal to come after me, and I just wanted to stay out of the courtroom. At least for a while. I took a seat, and I guess the sadness in my eyes shown because he asked, "So if you are done with the criminal system, what do you want to do?"

I bowed my head and said a quick prayer over my meal and then said, "Right at this very moment, I can't say Malice. But don't worry, I have some money saved, and I won't be a burden," I added.

He chuckled. "Baby, I am not for one moment worried about money or what you got. I am good, we are good, and I can take care of us."

"I know, but I still have a mortgage until my place is rented, and I have bills that I still have to handle."

He walked around and embraced me from behind. "And as I said, I got whatever you need. This building was about to be demolished, and Rel got it for pennies, so I don't have a mortgage... so I got you for whatever you need for as long as you need it. I don't want you to stress about anything Juicy. I got us, so please don't insult me. If you want to paint and draw all damn day, I will take care of everything. This weekend, we will sit and go over all your bills, and we will tackle them together, so don't stress, baby. I am a six-figure king, so my queen will never have to worry," he said and kissed the side of my face.

"That is extra kind of you baby, and my independent voice is screaming *girl, fuck that*, but my inner Gloria Jean is screaming, *let a man be a man*."

"Your mother is a wise woman. You can take some time off and decide what you wanna do, and in the meantime, I got you."

"Thank you, baby... you don't know how much that means to me."

"I'd do anything for you, Princess... now eat your dinner before it gets too cold," he suggested. I grabbed my fork and dug into the baked chicken, asparagus, and potatoes. After I was stuffed, I cleared the island and began to clean the kitchen while he went for Bistro's leash to take him out. That had become our evening routine, and I was glad that Malice was not devoting every second of his day to work. Sometimes, he kept late nights when it was absolutely necessary; but since the night of the incident with Silky, he made sure he was home before me or by the time I got off. After my shower, I got a text from Gabby.

Gab – SIS THE POLICE TOOK GUTTA TO THE STATION HOURS AGO AND I AM FREAKING OUT

Me – WHAT!

Gab – YES, CAN YOU AND MALICE COME OVER. I REALLY NEED YOU

Me – NO DOUBT, WE WILL BE THERE SHORTLY

"Babe," I called out.

"Yeah," he answered from the living room. I was in bed in my loungewear, surfing the net looking at possible new careers.

"We need to get to Gabby's. She said the police took Gutta to the station hours ago, and she wants us to come over."

"The fuck?" he questioned.

"I know," I said, closing my laptop. I got up to change. We rode to Gabby's while I was on the line with her. I convinced her that it would be okay to tell Gemma, Chas, and Tori, and she agreed. After I hung up, Malice and I dove right in with conversations about what was going on. We both suspected that Gutta had that bitch murdered, but we didn't know it for sure. We both agreed if that were the case, we'd never tell a soul. Other than our circle, no one would know because that bitch got exactly what she deserved for all the shit she had done. When we arrived, all the cars of my siblings and future in-laws were crowded in Gutta and Gabby's circular drive. We walked in and was greeted by hugs and kisses from our family, and when we were all in the family room, all eyes were on my sister. She swallowed all of the contents in her glass and then stood and went over to the kitchen to refill her glass. We were all quiet because I figured none of us knew what to say. She took another swallow.

"Listen, everything that everyone in this room is thinking is true. Trina had to go, so it is what the fuck it is," she declared, and none of us reacted.

"No one in this room will ever say a thing, you know that right?" I said.

She nodded. "I know. Everyone in this room loves us, so I ain't worried about any of us. I am just terrified of what the authorities might know or don't know. It's been hours, and I'm trying with everything to keep it together," she said and began to sob. We ladies all hurried over to her. The men let us comfort her.

"Gabby, please sis, don't worry. Gutta got this, and my brother is going to walk through that door at any moment. He would never do shit that would cause him to lose you and my niece, so don't cry sis," Royal said. I was surprised that he spoke up first, but when it came to his brothers, he was fearless.

She nodded. We led her over to the sofa, and we all stayed with her until after nine that night. When her phone rang, we were all relieved to know that Gutta was free to go. Rel and the other brothers convinced Gabby to let them go and pick up Gutta, and she finally gave in and stayed with us girls. "My husband is not a monster," she said. We all looked at her.

"What?" Gemma said.

"I just don't want any of you ladies to look at him differently. Gutta loves GiGi and me, and he took care of our problem."

We all started to speak at once, assuring her that that was the last thing we thought of her husband. Gutta made a hard decision I was sure of it. I don't know the details of what went through his mind to actually go through with it, but I was sure it was to protect my sister and niece. "Gabby, stop, okay. Just don't do this to yourself. We are your sisters and your best friends, and we are just as loyal as Rel,

Malice, and Royal. We are family, and I am glad Gutta took every measure to make sure you and GiGi are safe because if you want my truth, I'd say a million times over that I'd rather it be Trina than you," I said.

"Agreed," Chas chimed in.

"Absolutely big sis," Gemma added. We hugged and sat with my sister until our men walked in. Gabby raced into Gutta's arms, and I watched how tightly my brother-in-law held my sister as she cried in his arms.

"It's all good, baby, don't worry. We are good, I can assure you."

She looked up at him. "Are you positive, Gutta?" she questioned.

"I've been cleared, and I am not a suspect," he declared, and the cries that came out of my sister was a cry of relief. Malice grabbed my hand, and we all thought it was best to leave Gutta and Gabby alone. We exchanged hugs and kisses, and I love you's before leaving Gutta and Gabby's place. Before Malice helped me into his SUV, he pulled me into his arms.

He squeezed me tight and then said, "Let's set a wedding date. I am ready to call you, *my wife*."

I smiled up at him and just nodded. We agreed to wait at least a year, but like him, I figured it was no sense in delaying it. We were already living together, and I was more than sure that Malice was the one.

✿ 9 ✿

ROYAL

When I walked Gemma to her car, I didn't want to say goodnight. It had been a stressful evening, and I needed a drink, and something inside of me just yearned for her. I mean, shit was still new and early, and I knew she may not have wanted to open wide for me, but that is precisely what I had in mind for us that night. "So, what are you about to get into Miss lady?" I asked before I opened her door.

"Nothing but home. This has been an evening for sure, and I am hungry as hell."

"So, let's go for something to eat," I suggested.

"I came here straight from work, I don't want to go in my scrubs."

"Well, we can go to your place, and I can order something. And I need to stop and get me a bottle of Crown. Shit got so real today, and for a moment, I was a lil worried that they had something on my brother. I truly am grateful to God that there was nothing to associate him with that shit."

"Same here. I don't know how Gabby would make it if she lost Gutta behind Trina."

"I know, but let's get out of this cold. I can order and pick up something, babe."

"Okay," she said and slid in as soon as I opened her door.

"Is chicken good? I can hit up Harold's if that's cool with you."

"I can smash some Harold's. I want mild and hot sauce on my plate, and I am good with all wings please," she said.

"I got you beautiful. Drive safe, and I will be there soon," I said, about to shut her door, then I asked. "You need something from the liquor store?"

"Shit, you on that dark shit."

"It's whatever you want, though, bae. I got you," I assured.

"Cîroc, peach," she smiled, and I couldn't resist. I leaned in and kissed her lips, and she kissed me back. I backed away and shut her door, and headed to my Infinity. I headed toward the closest liquor store near Harold's and near Gemma's place. Before I could park, she texted, asking me to grab her an extra plate so she could have lunch for the next day. I texted back, saying *no problem,* and she replied that *she'd pay me back.* I sent back about five laughing emojis. I was still young, not even twenty-seven yet, but money has never been a problem for me. My parents did well, and by my third year of college, I had already owned three car washes. By my last year, Gutta, Malice, and Rel invested in my first detailing business. After three years in business, I was able to return their investments, and one thing about my family was that we didn't charge interest. I gave them exactly how much they put in, and a year after that, I had my second location. Again, my brothers stepped in and gave whatever I needed to get shit going, and even though I still owed that debt to them, there was no conflict because we did well. My oldest brother Gutta was the cause of us all being as successful as we were, and I honestly looked up to him for paving the way and being an example for us to all be independent businessmen.

I knew my brothers mostly saw me as the little brother that would never mature, but Gemma made me want to grow the fuck up and stop dipping and pimping. Bitches nowadays were not driven, and all you had to do was push a nice whip, have a nice crib, and treat them to VIP; and they'd sell their kids just to be a ho' ass dick pleaser. I had women to do all kinds of crazy shit for a few dollars and a night up in VIP poppin' bottles. They all were starting to look like a carbon copy of each other. The same tiny waist, fat ass, and perky tits that most may have taken their first loan out to achieve. They all wore the same beat face with long lace fronts or weaves and fake ass lashes that made them look like a supermodel. It was all superficial. When I laid eyes on Gemma, I was like *damn*, and she was a fucking RN. Yep, meaning she went to fucking school. Her hair was short, not weaved, and I didn't see her lashes and tits before I saw her. Her makeup was subtle and enhancing, not like she was preparing to be on the cover of someone's magazine, and I liked what I saw.

I had no intention of falling for her as soon as I had, but when she opened her smart-ass mouth, I was hooked. It was no use fighting it, and I'd be the last Wilkerson man to fall in love, marry, and maybe have kids with one of the Jackson sisters. My niece GiGi was the most adorable baby that I had ever laid eyes on, so I figured if Gutta and Gabby can produce someone so beautiful, Gemma and I would do the same.

I grabbed the largest bottle of Apple Crown and the largest bottle of Cîroc from the shelves and then paid. As soon as I got into my truck, I called Harold's and put our order in. I remembered to order an extra plate for Gemma, making sure to order only wings on both. I made sure to tell them to put the sauce on the side for one of them because I didn't want her order to be disastrously soggy with the sauce the next day. Once I had the packages, I hurried to my truck and then headed to Gemma's. I cranked my music, and my music stopped when a call from one of my regulars interrupted. I hit ignore, and within the next few seconds, she called again. I hit ignore again, then decided to put my phone on "do not disturb." I had been laying low lately, and there were nights when my phone would blow up all night since I had stopped answering.

I needed to honestly let them all know that I was seeing someone because some women just don't take the subtle hint of a nigga, never answering or responding. Some women continued to call relentlessly, and that shit was just crazy as hell to me. There were times when my brothers advised me to just tell a woman the truth, but I'd be like if a bitch crazy enough to keep blowing up my phone after so long of me not answering or responding, she damn sure wasn't going to stop because I said so. Shit, it only took a couple of times of being ignored for me to get the picture.

By the time I made it to Gemma's, my phone had stopped buzzing every two minutes. I still put it on "do not disturb" though after I parked. I sent her a quick text to let her know that I was there, and she texted back saying she was on her way down to help with the food and drinks. I was glad of that because I had a lot to carry up to her floor, and as fit, as I was, I did not want to make two trips. Once we were seated at the table with our plates in front of us, I couldn't keep my eyes off of her.

"What?" she questioned.

"You are just so damn pretty," I said. I knew it was a bit cheesy, but she was. Her scent led me to believe that she had already showered because she smelled fruity and had on a tank and some boy shorts. Her bronze skin glowed, and her face was make-up free but still looked fresh. On her head, she wore a black scarf, but I could gaze at her naturally beautiful face all night.

"Whatever, Royal," she said, clicking her tongue.

"No, I am so damn serious. You are like so radiant right now, and you are a very gorgeous woman Gemma."

She smirked. "Thank you, Royal," she said and then bit into a piece of chicken. She chewed slowly, eyeing me as if she didn't believe me, but then I smiled and winked at her.

"You're not so bad yourself," she said. I chuckled a bit and turned my attention to my plate. We ate and exchanged light conversation. Once we were done and cleaned a couple of dishes we had used, she fixed us both a drink. We ended up on her sofa. Once my sweater and Jordan's were off, we were relaxing, watching a movie. She was resting in my arms, and before long, her light snores invaded my ears. I wanted things to get more heated, but since she tapped out, I thought I'd help her to bed and then head home. I tapped her arm lightly to wake her.

"Gem, baby," I whispered. Her eyes fluttered as she looked up at me. "I should go, it's late," I said.

"No, please, I want you to stay," she said.

"Are you sure?"

She nodded. "Yes, please," she said, sitting up from resting in my arms. I followed her to her room, and it was familiar because I had shared her bed before. I took off my jeans and tossed them onto her chair and climbed into bed with her. I let her snuggle close to me, and when she pressed her plump ass against my dick, it stiffened. I couldn't control it. I wasn't embarrassed because Gemma turned me on, and I wanted her.

"Baby, can we?" I asked.

"Can we what?" she shot back.

I felt like a high schooler, but I said. "Can I feel you tonight?"

"You will, but not tonight," she said. Her words were soft, but they stung, and my dick deflated. I thought for a second. No one had ever told me *no* before, so that shit was new. I had never just shared a bed with a woman that I didn't smash, except for the first night I stayed over with Gemma, and that night I was cool with not hitting, but this night was another story.

"That's cool," I said. "Can I at least get a kiss?"

She turned over onto her back, and I leaned in, and she allowed me to kiss her deeply. Our tongues danced, and I loved kissing her. After a few moments, she broke the kiss. "I'm tired, baby, and have an early shift."

"Okay, babe, I will let you get some sleep." She turned back onto her side and pressed her ass back into me, and I held her close. My dick grew large again, but after twenty minutes of her soft snores, my eyes closed for good. The next morning, her alarm woke us both.

GEMMA

When I got to work the next morning, all thoughts were about Royal. I was falling for his lil arrogant ass, and I wondered if I could actually tolerate his ass long term or even in a serious relationship. Like, he never backed down from an argument, and he could outwit me on a bad day, and I didn't like that shit. I mean, his clever punch lines were impressive because, before Royal, no one could spar with me without walking away with his tail between his legs. My daddy used to tell me that if I hadn't gone into the nursing field, I'd make a damn good comedian, and I agreed. I was always the funny animated one of my sisters. I always stole the crowd with my humor, slick comebacks, smart mouth, and ability to clap back quickly. I got that spirit from Gloria Jean, and most everyone agreed that I was just like her.

"Gemma, the patient in 2A, needs help going to the bathroom," Dr. Reed said, interrupting my thoughts.

"Ummm, there are no CNA's on deck, Dr. Reed? I am a little busy with 4C and 3A. Dr. O'Neal has already given me a task to complete," I said as politely as I could. I could not stand Dr. Reed's old funky breath ass. He was always so super friendly to me in the beginning until I realized his kindness came with a proposition. I had heard from other nurses how he'd make advances, and since he had never advanced on me, I didn't have a problem with his kind gestures.

He never gave me a hard time until one late night. I was doing a night shift, and that night was oddly quiet for Mercy. So, we were all pretty much chillin' and wondering off to get away from the ER. I was in a smaller waiting room area, playing around on my phone when he approached. We were always cool, professional, and cordial, so I had no problems with him taking a seat across from me.

"Enjoying this quiet night?" Dr. Reed asked after he sat.

"I am. The change of pace is so welcomed, and one work night a week like this would be awesome," I said.

He smiled, and it wasn't flattering because Dr. Reed was not a very attractive man. He was in his mid-fifties, I guessed, and for him to be a doctor, his damn mouth was fucked all the way up. He smelled like an expensive cologne with an after taste of funk breath, and I hated to be too close to his ass. His teeth were the color of coffee-stained brown, and I figured his wife left because she couldn't stomach the sight of his deteriorating mouth.

"So, if you were off tonight, what would you be doing?"

"Most likely out with my sisters and girlfriends. They are at Cooper's Hawk right now, and I'd love to be there with them."

"I'm sure," he said, and his gaze made me feel a little uncomfortable, so I stood.

"Well, Doc, I should head back, just in case I am missing some action."

"Okay, but wait, I wanna ask you one more thing."

I paused and nodded. "Sure, doc, you can ask me anything."

"Are you sure because what I want to ask you is a little on a personal note?"

Curious, I said, "No worries. We are both adults."

"I was wondering if I could fuck you?"

The question made my mouth open, but nothing came out at first, but then the Gloria Jean in me kicked in, and I smirked. "With all due respect, Dr. Reed, fuck no!" I said and rolled my eyes at that old funky breath bastard. I was insulted but wasn't surprised. After that night, he stopped treating me with the same kindness and courtesy that he had shown me before, and I was okay with that. I didn't care what the fuck he thought, and I made it a point to pull out my phone and hit record every time he and I were in a space alone. If he felt he could sexually harass me again, I'd have his funky breath ass on tape.

Now I stood before him with a look of defiance on my face, and I knew he knew better than to tell me again to go to a room to help a patient to the damn toilet. I did on many occasions if I had too, but I wasn't going to do shit he told me too.

"Fine, I will locate a CNA. If she pisses the bed, someone is going to have to clean it up," he shot.

"And that someone won't be me," I said and moved on. Dr. Reed could eat a dick as far as I was concerned. I finished up with my other two patients and went back to the nurse's station. I checked my phone, and I had a few messages from Royal, so I smiled and replied. I was feeling him, yes, but I didn't know why something inside of me wanted to play hard to get. I wanted his ass, but Royal was so damn conceited, and I didn't want to make it easy for him. I wanted him to not so much work for it, but just for him to know that he couldn't get it so damn easy.

I finished out my shift and told Royal that I'd see him Friday night. We hooked up, but that night, I shut him down when he tried to get some. I wanted to, but like I said, he wasn't going to get my good, good so damn quickly. We got together several nights, and I still hadn't given him the goods. He'd stay over and hold me, and I enjoyed that shit. It had been four weeks of him doing everything that I like, and I had fallen for his ass for real. It was a Wednesday of that fifth week, and I just wanted to go home, shower, eat, and sleep. I could not let his big ass dick rest on my ass because I'd give in for sure if he were in my bed again that night. The night before, he had slept over again. I wanted to suck and fuck his ass, but I was glad Mr. Sandman came through and made my ass too tired to move.

By Friday, I was grateful, and even though I had planned to go out that night with my peeps and Royal, I was so damn exhausted. I figured I'd go home after work and take a little nap, but when I woke, it was after eleven. I had worked seven till seven that day, and when I looked at my phone, I had several messages from Royal. "Fuck!" I said and hurried out of my bed. I rushed to take a shower and hurried to get dressed. By the time I finally made it to Desire, it was close to twelve-thirty. When I made it to VIP, the crew was there, but my head tilted when I saw another chick damn near sitting in Royal's lap. I looked at Grace, and she hunched her shoulders.

I spoke to everyone and took a seat by Grace and Malice. Gabby and Gutta were not in VIP, nor did I see Rel and Chas, but I recognized Gabby's handbag on the seat, so I knew they were somewhere around. I quickly fixed a drink as I eyed Royal and wondered who in the fuck was he with when all he had been trying to do was make me all his. When he finally looked my way, I rolled my eyes, and he smirked at me. *This muthafucka*, I thought and then threw back my drink. I poured another, and Chas and Rel came in and sat on the other side of Royal and his bitch ass friend. She was pretty enough, slim, perky tits, long laced front, and long lashes. *Her face would have been pretty without the make-up,* I thought, as I examined her beautiful features, and I had to admit that shit to myself. My only question was, why would he entertain this bitch when he pretended to be so into me? I mean, he must have really thought I wasn't coming to do some old goofy-ass shit like that in front of my damn sisters when they knew that Royal and I had something going on.

I sat there on one muthafuckin' hundred and hated that this muthafucka had gotten to me. My *usual me* would have given him the finger, rolled my eyes, and went to find me a man to entertain, but my *post feelings for Royal me* stood and said, "Raphael, can I holla at you for a minute?" All eyes were on me, and I knew why because I was sure no one expected me to use his government name or to make a scene.

"Gemma, bring all that shit down... it is not that serious, for real babe, just have a seat," he said.

Have a seat, I thought to myself and wanted to dive onto his ass. "Royal?" I said, crossing my arms across my breasts.

"Who dis?" the dizzy ass other woman asked with a scowl on her face. I knew she was confused.

She had no clue that she was sitting with my entire fam, so she was out of order. "Bitch, you need to stay in yo' fuckin' lane and close yo' muthafuckin' mouth," I blasted. I already knew that I was being so damn extra, but Royal was about to pour water on the flames inside of me that just had started for his ass. I liked him. I mean, I really, really liked him and wanted him, but this bullshit was pissing me the fuck off.

"Bitch!" she snapped.

"Aye, aye, aye!" Rel yelled with authority. "Royal, escort your little friend to another table, and Gemma, please take a seat."

Rel wasn't my daddy or my brother-in-law, but because he was married to Chas, I had mad respect for him, so I obliged. Royal got his stupid ass up and took his little bitch to whatever table; and when he came back without her, he sat beside me. I was furious and didn't even look at his ass. I just kept sipping my drink and rolling my damn eyes.

"I'm sorry, Gem," he said, leaning in close to me.

"Fuck you!" I shot back at him.

"That chick doesn't mean shit to me," he said, getting even closer to me. I wanted to punch his ass, but at the same time, I wanted him to lean in closer to me. I wanted to feel the heat of his breath on my ear because I wanted him and had fallen for him.

"Why did you have her over here with our family Royal? I mean, if you still fucking chicks, do you. But you got me and everyone else thinking that you are feeling me and shit, but I walk in, and you got her hanging with our peeps, what the fuck?"

"First, I thought you weren't coming Gem. I called and texted and shit. I met her, she seemed cool, and I didn't want to be sitting up in my brothers' faces with their women by myself, so I brought her over. When you walked in, I couldn't just dismiss her. Look, I had no intention of leaving with her, hooking up with her, or anything like that. I just invited her for the company."

I believed him, but the sight of him with another woman pissed me the fuck off. "So, you are saying you can't party with our fam without a woman? I mean, sometimes I work nights and can't be here, so you just have to have another woman entertain you?"

"No, but you keep turning me off and on Gemma. I am doing all I can to be close to you, but you give me excuses, put me off and shit. You know I am feeling you, and you know I want your ass, but you let me lay in your bed with my dick on brick, and I am a man. If you want me like I want you, you have to show me that shit too, Gemma. I want to do this shit with you, but all the hot and cold bullshit is lame as fuck. And if you wanna keep playing these bullshit ass games, I can move around. I mean, it's been damn six, almost seven weeks since the wedding. I wine and dine you. I rub your damn feet and do all the things that a man is supposed to do, but all I've gotten is kisses. I need and want to do this with you, Gemma. If you let me, I will be so damn good to you. I want you so fucking bad baby," he said, talking into my ear.

I nodded. I agreed with him, and I leaned into him. "I do want you too, Royal, and I am sorry for the little waiting game that I've played with you, okay. When I walked in and saw that bitch sitting so close to you, I wanted to jump her ass. I am sorry for giving you mixed signals, baby. I do want you." I confessed.

"So, you're going to give me some of that pussy tonight?" he breathed into my ear.

I touched his thigh and then nodded with a smile. "Yes, baby, tonight, you can have all of me." He turned my face to him and kissed me so deeply right in front of everyone as if no one was around. We partied more with our family, and that was the first night I left my car and went to his place. It was definitely a bachelor's pad, but it was comfortable enough for me. He showed me around, and it was beautiful. I didn't stop him from kissing me. We started in his living room before we made our way to his bedroom.

Never on the first encounter did I do or even care for oral because, as a nurse, I was always super cautious; but when his tongue stroked my bulb, I spread my legs as far apart as I could. He ate my pussy so fucking good that my core erupted more juices than I had ever produced before. The lower half of my body trembled uncontrollably, and I called on Jesus when my orgasm hit me. He came up, licking and sucking on my skin. When he made it to my tits, he ravished them so thoroughly, and so skillfully, I'd thought I cream again. He rubbed his rod against my center as he pleased my mounds, but I wanted him to put on the plastic. "Royal, condom, please... put on a condom," I panted. He pulled back, went into his nightstand drawer, and then pulled out a box. It was a large box, but when a long line of condoms rolled from the box, I felt a little relieved that the box was more full than empty.

After he was protected, he climbed back on top of me and kissed me deeply as he guided the head of his dick to my center. I moved the lower half of my body to meet up with his, and he pushed himself inside of me. I don't know what it was, but every inch of Royal made my pussy clench, and I got wetter and wetter for him. We changed positions, and that shit was so fucking good, I had multiples. I swore to never suck a dick without clinical proof of being STD free, but Royal had his dick down my throat within hours of me being had his place. We had literally fucked all night because he could last forever, and three condoms and countless orgasms later, the sun was coming up. We both cuddle close as we could and fell into a sound sleep.

❧ 11 ❧

ROYAL

When I peeped at the clock, it was afternoon. My baby's body was draped over mine, and if I didn't have to piss, I would have not disturbed my sleeping angel. I slid out of bed, and she didn't even open an eyelid. I went to the bathroom and brushed my teeth after I washed my hands. I went to the kitchen and opened my fridge, and since I wasn't a cook, that motherfucker was pretty much bare, except for Styrofoam containers of some old ass takeout. I cringed and knew I had to dress and go out to get us something to eat. I went to my bedroom, and once I confirmed that Gemma was still sound asleep, I threw on some sweats and a hoodie. I stepped into my J's, and even though it was early April, it was still chilly as fuck outside, so I grabbed my Bears jacket.

Since it was afternoon, I figured I'd go for some lunch instead of breakfast, so I went by a sub joint and grabbed us a couple of ham, turkey, and roast beef combinations with some salt and vinegar chips. I remember those tiny details about my baby over the weeks as I observed her routine, and remembered the things she said that she loved and the things she strongly disliked. I got her a pineapple Crush and me a Pepsi because that was my go-to pop. When I put my car in gear, my phone alerted me of a text.

Mean Ass – WHERE R U BABY?

Me – I RAN OUT 2 GET SOME GRUB. IS EVERYTHING OKAY?

Mean Ass – YES, JUST WOKE UP TO AN EMPTY BED, HURRY BACK

Me – I AM ON MY WAY BABE

I pulled out and rode the short distance back to my place. When I walked in, I put the food on the counter and headed to the bedroom, and my bed was empty. I heard water running, and I knew Gemma was in the shower. I figured she had found the linen closet, so I headed back to the main living area and grabbed the remote. I turned on the tube and went straight to HGTV. If we're not watching movies, that is the channel my baby watched or the cooking network. I went into my kitchen and took our sandwiches from the bag and got a couple of plates. I filled two glasses with ice, and when she came out in one of my Chicago Cubs t-shirts and a pair of my Polo boxers, I knew she had gone through my drawers. "I see you found your way around," I said, putting our plates on the island.

"Yes, I found something to be comfortable in, I hope you don't mind," she said and took a seat at the island.

"Nah, it's cool. I don't have shit to hide, so you good."

"Okay," she smiled.

"Do you want your sandwich heated?" I asked.

"Nah, I like it cold," she smiled. I hurried to put the chips and drinks onto the island. I had to rush around and kiss her. She was so damn cute, and I wanted to just love on her ass all the damn time.

"Me too," I added then went around the island. I embraced her from behind and planted a few kisses on her neck, nuzzling my nose against her neck to inhale her scent. She tilted her head to the left, giving full access to her neck and collarbone. I kissed her softly a few times before I took a seat. "Gem, you are so damn intoxicating baby," I expressed as I pulled my plate of food closer to me.

"So are you, Royal, and last night baby was amazing," she said, smiling.

"It was, baby, and trust, my dick cannot wait to dig into your sweet center again. Yo' shit is like a gushy soft pillow," I said, trying to describe the feelings that she had given my pole as best as I could.

"Wow," she giggled. "I am glad you enjoyed me because I damn sure enjoyed you, baby," she said and then took a bite of her sandwich. We chatted and talked about the events that went down the night before, and after we ate, I went to shower. We lounged on the sofa for a while, and we ended up in bed again. We fucked the entire evening until we got a text from Malice saying to meet them over at his place. It was a Saturday evening, and we'd typically patronize one of my brothers' clubs, but Malice said he just wanted us to come over to his place. We'd play pool, cards, and just hang.

When I told Gemma, she was down, but she had to go to her place to get something else to wear. I told my big bro that we'd come through, and then we headed to Gemma's. She took another shower and dressed while I watched some bullshit that was on MTV. When she was set, we decided to go in my truck and come back to her place after.

"So, are we together, together now?" I asked her.

"What do you mean, Royal?"

"You know what the fuck I mean, Gem. We are like too old to be saying we are boyfriend and girlfriend, but I do want to call you *my woman* and be *your man*."

She giggled. "Yes, I am officially *your* woman, and you are now *my* damn man."

"Dat's what the fuck is up." I was grinning hard as a muthafucka, and I was not ashamed. I had finally found the first woman that I wanted to claim as all *mine*, and I was excited to see how far Miss Mean Ass and I would go.

Once we got to Malice and Grace's place, we parked, and I hurried to help my baby out of the car. She was impressed by my brother's place, and I was so surprised that that was her first time there. Once inside, the entire Wilkerson clan and their wives were there, including Tori and her husband. We did a few quick introductions because I had never met her husband and a night of fun with games, drinks, and our ladies got underway.

❧ 12 ❧

CHAS

I looked down at the test, and when it was negative, I didn't try to hold back my tears. It had only been four months since I had said I do, and even though I said I'd wait six months to seek medical treatment, I had a change of heart. I was so anxious and desperate to give my husband a baby that I had started going to his mother's church. Yes, I believed in God all my life, but I wasn't a regular church-goer, not until I really wanted God to give me and my husband a mira-cle. I spent so much time thinking of not being able to have kids, I had to see someone before I went insane. I just had to know the verdict. I had to know if something was wrong, and I couldn't sit around on my hands and wait another damn day to know what was really going on.

As soon as Rel walked through the door, I met him. "Baby, I think we should schedule an appointment to see why I can't get pregnant," I said.

He chuckled. "Well, good evening Mrs. Wilkerson. How was your day baby? Mine was good."

I exhaled. "Baby, I am so sorry. Welcome home," I said, giving my husband a wet kiss. "My day was fine as far as work, the girls, and all, but I took the test, and again it was negative."

He started to remove his leather jacket. "I thought we agreed to give it six months, Chas, and I told you not to take that test until you missed your cycle," he said, going for the coat closet.

"I know what we said, Rel, but this baby business is driving me insane, and I am obsessing on it. If I don't get the answers I need, I am going to stress even more about it, and I am sure that the stress is not helping."

He nodded and shut the closet door after hanging his jacket. "I know it's not and listen, babe, my love, my everything..." he said, tenderly caressing my cheek. "I told you that I want a child, but it's not urgent. And if we can't have them, I am still going to adore you, and we can still live a full life without kids," he reiterated.

My head dropped. I knew my husband was one thousand percent right, but I didn't want to hear that. I leaned in and put my head on his chest as he held me. "Rel, I know, but now I really want to be a mom. Things were so fucked up with Chris that I never thought about kids again after I miscarried. Then I met you, fell in love all over, and this time so damn deeply that I want a part of you. I want a part of us to love on and spoil and even drives us crazy. I see Gabby with GiGi and Tori with little EJ, and I want that for us."

He released me and cupped my chin. "I know, babe, and I do too, so if you want to scratch the six-month plan, we can do that. It's whatever makes you happy, babe." Rel said tenderly.

I loved him so damn much for loving me so much. I smiled at my husband before I kissed him. I wrapped my arms around his neck and held him as tight as I could. "Thank you, baby, for being so wonderful to me. I know that this is real, I know what we have is real, babe... but sometimes, I do have to pinch myself to make sure that I'm not dreaming because the day I divorced Chris, I never knew that this would be my reality. You have been so damn good to me, and sometimes, I feel like I don't show you just how much I love and appreciate you."

He pulled away. "Baby, you just keep doing exactly what you have been doing. I can't take all of the credit because, before you, I never saw this for me either. A new wife, having kids, all of the things that I thought for a very long time that I'd never have, and then you came along, sexier than a muthafucka, and put the heat on me and I lost my damn mind," he joked.

I blushed. "You always have to go there, don't you?" I said because Rel always teased me about how fiyah my pussy was that I made him want to give me his last name.

"Yes, I do because it's true, babe. Now your man is hungry. I had a long day at Malice with his picky ass fiancée, so I need a cold one and a hot meal."

I scrunched my nose and said, "I am sorry, baby, I didn't cook. I got home and went straight up to take that stupid test."

"Damn, babe... I mean, you slipping," he teased as I followed him to the kitchen.

"I know, and I am sorry. I know it was my turn, but I can call and order something for you. I'll even run out and get it, so we don't have to worry about delivery."

He went and opened the fridge and grabbed a beer. "Sounds good, so by the time I'm done showering, you should be back," he said, popping the top on his beer and taking a swig.

"Yep, I should be," I said and reached for my phone. "What are you in the mood for?"

"My wife's cooking," he joked.

"Man, besides that," I said.

"An Italian combo will work."

"Cool," I said and called a lil restaurant not far from us that sold Gyros, Chicago Style Hot Dogs, and other stuff like wings, fish, and pizza puffs. I hurried to pick up our food, and he hurried up to shower. When I got into the car, I called Gabby.

"Hey, babe, what's crackin'?" she answered cheerfully.

"Damn, you are in a good mood."

"I am... my husband just licked me to the most amazing orgasm before he left to take GiGi to my mother's for the weekend."

"But Gab, it is Thursday," I said.

"It most certainly is, but Gloria Jean and Boris don't get up before seven, so dropping her off in the morning on my way to school wouldn't work, so momma said to bring GiGi tonight."

"Okayyyyyyy," I dragged out. "What is the occasion? Why are you and Gutta getting rid of the baby for the weekend? Y'all got some special plans or something?"

"Other than setting the world record for the most orgasms in a seventy-two-hour period, we have a couple's spa day, dinner at Steak 48, a couple's cooking lesson... let's see that wine and paint thing, we just plan to do us this weekend. No Passions or Desire or sisters, brothers, or friends."

"Well damn, I see. Y'all must be planning to give GiGi a damn sister or brother?"

"Hell, we might because I plan to fuck and suck so many times this weekend that I won't be able to walk straight or swallow for a damn week."

"Ohhh shit... yo' ass is nasty."

"Only with my husband, so it's all good, baby," she said, and I loved hearing the upbeat manner in her tone. Hell, maybe that's what Rel and I needed. I knew we just had a honeymoon, but perhaps a weekend in a nice hotel with a change of scenery could get our baby juices flowing.

"I know that is real girl, and speaking of babies, I called to tell you that Rel and I decided to seek infertility now instead of waiting for another two months."

"Well, if you feel like it's time, I say go for it. I mean, life is so full of surprises and what-ifs and there is no time to waste on being happy. Being a mother is tiring as fuck, I won't lie, but I love that kid with every ounce of my being."

"I hear that."

"Yes ma'am, and I will pray that it's nothing going on with your body Chas. I know there are other ways to become parents, but I can totally understand that instinct inside of you to carry your own baby; however, keep in mind that there is a mother out there that came to be a mother through other ways... rather she is an adopting mother, or family member who took in a kid to raise it, or a grandparent that stepped in. Just remember that you don't have to push one out to still have that bond."

I smiled as I pulled into the parking lot of the restaurant. "I know Gab, and if there is anything that will prevent me from getting pregnant, I know there is a child or few out there that Rel and I can love and spoil just as much."

"Indeed, but let me get off of this phone and go shower and get ready for round two of my night with my man before he gets back here."

"Al'ight babe, have fun."

"I most definitely will," she cooed into the phone, and we ended the call. I parked, got out, and went inside to grab our take-out. When I got home, I suggested that we do something romantic that weekend too, but Rel reminded me of the extra projects for Gracie that he had going on at Malice's place. I pouted a little and then called Grace. I expressed to her that my man needed that weekend to tend to me, and she agreed that he could skip that one weekend if he needed to. I went online and scoped out some luxury hotels, booking the first one that had a Jacuzzi in the room. I was so grateful that I stopped working on Saturdays after I got married, so there was no need to reschedule any of my clients. I informed my husband of our new plans, and we spent the rest of our evening on the sofa with foot rubs, wine, and a movie.

❦ 13 ❧

GEMMA

It was June, and the folks in Chicago were all in full clown mode. The hospital was always busier because there were more shoot-ings, more fights, and all kinds of stabbings. The heat apparently made mofo's lose their damn minds, and I had been working more than pleasing my man. It had been four months, and our thing was so good. I had such deep feelings for Royal and was starting to believe that he was truly the one. Trust, I had my doubts in the beginning because he was such an ass from day one, but I was watching him transform into a mature man like his older brothers. There were hardly any sparring matches between us, but when we were with the family, he and his brothers would all crack on each other about something or another.

When Royal decided to give me the *girlfriend* status, he gave me a key and re-introduced me to his parents as *his lady*. I remembered his mother smart-ass comment that another Jackson woman had hooked her son, but he reminded her that we were all the perfect match for him, Gutta, and Malice. Her evil ass cracked a half-smile and said, "As long as my boys are happy, I'm happy." I wanted to tell her that it was that Jackson pussy that had her boys all lost and turned out, but I refrain from saying that shit. Because if she was anything like Gloria Jean, I might have gotten popped in my smart-ass mouth.

I gazed at my Apple watch to recheck the time, and it was only eleven minutes after eight. I wanted so badly to get the hell up out of there, and I could not wait to see my man. Most times, Royal's day ended so much earlier than mine, so he would always have food waiting on me as soon as I walked in the door. Oddly, we spent more time at his place because it was a little closer to the hospital than mine, and he tended to have a little bit more activities going on at his place. Like friends over and employees hanging at his place. I never minded any of it because I went to sleep as soon as my head hit the pillow most nights, and I slept so soundly that his company never bothered me. There were a couple of mornings where his good friend Tas would be over with one of his side chicks, and although I didn't like that Tas was always keeping bitches on the side when he lived with a woman, that shit wasn't any of my damn business, so I never even voiced my opinions to Rel.

By the time my shift ended, I was dog tired. Royal insisted that I go by his place because he had company over, but I told him company was a fucking no for me because I wanted my tub, wine, and bed. Royal said he'd be by my place that night after he cleared out his company, and I was good with that. I clocked out and then headed to my car. When I got to the waiting area to vacate the building, someone called out my name, causing me to pause in my tracks.

I turned to lay eyes on Drew. He was a very familiar face because I remembered eyeing him at the wedding rehearsal, wedding, and reception. *Still gorgeous*, I thought and then quickly reminded myself that I was in a relationship with Royal. "Hey, hey, hey, you," I fumbled over my words a bit.

"Hey, yourself, Miss Gemma. I thought that was you. I actually can't believe I am running into you here."

"Well, I work here, and I am just getting off. What brings you to the ER?" I quizzed.

"It's my grandfather. He was having difficulty breathing, so the family brought him in. I just walked in like a minute ago and was talking to my cousin and saw you walking by."

"Yeah, well, I had a long ass day. Worked a double, and I am ready to get as far away from this hospital as I possibly can," I said, trying not to gaze. I had a man, but what stood before me was a man that I could see, giving me tall and caramel covered sons. Everything about him was beautiful, even the white teeth that sat behind his juicy ass dark pink lips. *You are with fine ass, dick slanging Royal*, I reminded myself again and decided to cut our conversation short. Drew was damn sure easy on the damn eyes, but I had a man that I honestly was digging; so Drew was only eye candy for me because I was happy with who I was with.

"I feel you, and I don't want to take up too much of your time. I just was wondering if you were maybe free for coffee, dinner, or cock-tails anytime soon? We met at the wedding, and Rel's brother pretty much staked a claim on you, so I didn't have an opportunity to get too close to you."

I wanted to say "for real dude?" when I saw you hollering at multiple women at the reception. There were times when Royal wasn't anywhere to be found, but Mr. Sexy was working his way around the room. Suddenly, that shit had come back to me. We had locked eyes a couple of times, and if he was really interested, fuck what Royal was on, he would have made a damn move anyway, so I said, "You know what? Royal and I are together now, and we have been since the night of the wedding, so I'm good, but thanks."

"Oh, so he did wear you down?"

"Wear me down? What are you talking about?"

"Nothing. I just heard that he was busy chasing while you were busy giving him the finger."

"Well back then, that was true, but it didn't take him long to lock me down. I was always interested, but a girl has to play a little hard to get," I said. Royal wasn't no soft ass begging nigga, so I didn't want him to think my man got me by default.

"Really, well you could have fooled me."

"Yeah, well, we're together now and trust he is not sorry that he chased because it was definitely worth it." My man was not a thirsty skirt-chasing bitch, so Drew had to know that our cat and mouse game was just what we needed. "Bottom line, he captured his prey, and we good."

"Okay, I feel you, Miss Gemma, you have a great night," he said, backing away.

"You the same, Mr. Drew," I returned. I hurried out of the automatic doors and hurried to my car. I got in, and once I was out of the hospital parking lot, I called Royal. That encounter with Drew made me miss him even more.

"Yo' lil momma, what's good?" he answered.

"Please tell me that you are on your way, baby. I like miss you in the worst way, and I want you there when I get home."

"I miss you too, babe, but are you okay? Is something wrong?"

"No, nothing is wrong. I just... I... I... I... I love you, Raphael. I just love you," I said first and for the first time.

"Aww, boo, I love you too, babe, and I am on my way," he said, and I heard the smile in his voice. I was happy with him, and my heart always skipped a beat for him. I waited for him to say *I love you* first, but since he hadn't, I couldn't hold on to the words anymore because that was indeed how I felt about him.

"Okay, babe, I can't wait to see you."

"Same baby, drive safely, and I will be there in a few minutes," he said, and then we ended the call. I drove home with my stomach doing flips, and I couldn't wait to see him.

14

ROYAL

I stuff my phone into my pocket and then walked back into my living room to my staff that was hanging out. "Okay, now, errrrbody got to get the hell up outta here. You ain't gotta go home, but y'all know the rest," I declared. They all grumbled and groaned as they stood to get their jackets, but my best friend Tas didn't budge. He and the hot chick he was with just stayed rooted on the sectional. "Tas, my man, it's time to beat it. My lady is off, and I need to head to her crib," I said, and he hopped up.

"Yo' Royal, let me holla at you for a second," he said, pushing me back towards my bedroom.

"Tas, dude, the fuck man?" I asked.

"Listen, Royal... man, I've been trying to hit for about five months, please let me stay and handle this. I will lock up, you know me. I would never disrespect yo' place bro, and this bitch can do splits, so please don't deny this... man, I'm begging you."

Tas always used my spot to cheat, and although I didn't like the shit he was on, he was my dude since grammar school, so I allowed him to stay.

"Look, man, do yo' business and get the hell up outta my crib. And in the guest room. Don't let this bitch roam around my place," I ordered.

"Royal, dude, I got you, and I know the damn rules, nigga, damn!" he replied. I headed to my woman's place, and even though it was late, I ran up in the twenty-four-hour Jewels to get her some damn flowers. I had wanted to tell Gemma that I loved her for days, but I was afraid she'd laugh or clown me. I felt it between us, but Gemma was just so damn spicy and feisty, I found myself treading lightly whenever I was with her. She didn't scare me or no shit like that, but I was so into her. My mission was to always see her happy, smiling, and in a good mood, so I pretty much stopped talking trash to her and made it a point to always compliment her, ask her what she was feeling, and how was her day going. I just always and truly wanted to make sure she was okay.

Gemma worked so damn hard, and if I had my way, I'd make her leave that stressful job; however, she told me that all her life she dreamed of being a nurse. When she was a little girl, she had broken her arm when she fell out of a tree. Gemma said that she met this nurse named Nurse Denise that was so nice to her and her patients that she just wanted to be like her. She also said that when she went in to have her tonsils removed, she had another nurse, Nurse Pam, and her experience with those two nurses told her early on what she wanted to be and what she wanted to be like. She worked hard, no doubt, but I loved her drive. And if I were her husband, I'd do double duty to make sure every waking moment that she didn't spend in the hospital on her feet helping others would be stress-free. I would see to it that she'd never had a problem or care, and I'd take care of her.

I got up and rushed up the stairs, and as soon as I walked in, she ran into my arms, almost knocking me over. I wrapped my free arm around her and kissed the top of her head.

"I missed you so much today," she exhaled.

"I missed you too, baby," I said, holding her as tight as she held me.

"I just want to be with you," she expressed.

"I only want to be with you too, baby, what's wrong? I mean, you are extra emotional tonight. Did something happen? Is the family good? Talk to me, baby, tell me what's really going on. I have never seen you this emotional, Gem. Baby, what happened?" I questioned.

She let me go and stepped back. "I ran into Drew, the guy that works for Rel and was in their wedding."

"I am very familiar with who Drew is, baby. Now tell me what happened?"

"Nothing major. It's just that we were talking, and he just... I don't know Royal... was just talking like you were some sorta chump or some thirsty ass nigga, and it like pissed me off. I mean, I am not sure what or why, but he made me want to punch him in the face because he doesn't know what we got or how great you are. I can't explain it, babe, but it just gave me this overwhelming feeling to protect *you*, to protect *us*, and I knew I had to tell you how I felt about you. I have been loving you for a little while now, but I was hoping you'd say it first. I know it's childish and petty, but I felt that if I said it first and you didn't say it back that I'd look like a fool."

I put the flowers down. "You and I are *exactly* the same and made for each other because I fell in love with you two weeks ago, but I was also afraid to just say it. I love you so damn much, Gemma, and I only wanna be with you. You are *my heart*, babe," I said. She walked back into my embrace, looking at me and smiling.

"You own *my heart*, Mr. Wilkerson."

"And I will take extra special care of it."

"You, betta," she shot.

"There is my lil mean ass," I said and kissed her passionately. We headed straight for her bedroom, and we made love for the rest of the night. The next day, I went home and grabbed a few items before going back over to Gemma's. She convinced me to go to church that Sunday. When I got there and saw Gutta and Malice, I figured Dee-Dee had no idea that her sons were at the Jackson's church and not hers. I knew Rel and Chas attended her church, but she'd slap Gutta, Malice, and me like we were the *Three Stooges*. That was the first time I heard my Gemma sing. When she did a song with her sister Grace, I had to keep wiping my eyes so that my big brothers wouldn't see me cry. Her voice touched something inside of me, and I knew I'd have to have a meeting with my brothers because I was ready to buy a damn ring.

When we got to Ms. Gloria Jean's house for our first Sunday

dinner, Malice and Gutta schooled me on how to not mentioned the girls' church services to my mother. My mother and I were close, and I felt like I didn't want to keep that secret from her, but my brothers threaten to whip my ass, so I quickly told them that I'd keep it on the low. We went back to Gemma's for a while before heading to my mom's for an evening dinner. We got it in one more time before we headed out. At Dee-Dee's on Sundays with the family was always lovely because lil GiGi turned my mother into mush. Even if you were on her list to be told, GiGi made my mother melt like butter left out on the porch in July.

It was getting late, so we were leaving to head home. Gutta and Gabby had gone a little earlier, and Malice and Grace left after Grace helped momma clean up. Gemma and I were in the living room with my dad, watching recorded episodes of his favorite show *Blackish*, and even though I was ready to go home so I could get all up inside of Gemma's treasure box, she and my Pops kept watching episode after episode. She and my daddy got along so well, and I could tell he had a different relationship with Gem than he had with Gabby, Chas, and Grace. None of them just really hung around my Pops like Gem.

"Ralph," my mom called out, and we all looked in her direction.

"Yes, ma'am," I answered.

"Can you come in here, son? I need to chat with you for a moment or two."

I stood. "Of course, yes ma'am," I said, moving quickly in her direction.

"Gemma, I won't keep him long. I know it's late."

"No, it's fine, Mrs. Wilkerson, I am happy right here with Pops watching Blackish." My mother nodded, and we went out to the sunporch off the kitchen and sat.

"What's up, momma?"

"You in love, son?" she asked me.

I put my head down but quickly lifted it. I was a grown ass man, and yes, I was in love. "Yes, momma, I am. Gemma is the one."

"How do you know this, Ralph? You are my baby, and you are so young. What type of voodoo or satanic spell are these Jackson women doing to my sons?"

I wanted to laugh, but I contained my laughter because my mother was serious. "Mother, listen, there is no voodoo, or hoodoo, or no spells. Gemma is feisty, outspoken, and could use a mussel at times, I will admit, but she is so smart and intelligent, and she works hard, ma. She is a God-fearing sister, and to tell you the truth, I went to church with her today." Dee-Dee's mouth dropped opened. "Yes, mother, I did, and she has a voice that will blow your mind. She loves God, and she loves *me,* ma. You always told us that you wanted us to marry a good girl. Gemma is a good girl, ma. Just like Gabby, Grace, and Chas. God has answered your prayers and gave you four God-fearing, loving daughters-in-law."

"I only have *two* daughters-in-law, and Grace will be my next one. You know you wanna marry Gemma already, son? You are so young, and you have time."

"I know, ma, but I know she is it. I don't know when I will pop the question, but to be honest, I am going ring shopping."

She nodded, and her eyes welled. "I guess I did a helluva job with you boys and you are right, God sent me four beautiful daughters-in-law, and all I want from y'all is a host of grandbabies. Hell, Bernadine got seven now, and I only have one... y'all boys need to not only catch up but give me more than seven. I mean them little monsters ain't even cute, and if the rest of my precious grandchildren come out as half as gorgeous as GiGi, all of them will be jealous."

I stood. "I love you, ma, and please let me and Malice get to the altar first. Chas and Rel will be giving you one soon because I know they are trying."

"Yes, and God is going to bless Chas' womb with three babies. I know this because God showed me this in a dream, and she is going to have children," she declared. I never questioned Dee-Dee's visions or prophecies because I genuinely didn't understand or know what that was all about; but, I believed her because I was sure she and God were on the same team. Growing up, she'd tell me things that will happen, and I didn't believe it until it happened, so if she said Chas and Rel would have three kids, I believed her.

"Well, ma, we are going to head out. If I let Gemma, she will sit here with Pops all night watching that show."

She stood and gave me a hug. "Good luck to you son, and even though I'd prefer you to attend my church, I'd rather you go to Gemma's than not go at all. So, I will let it slide that you chose to go to her church."

"Thanks, ma," I said, squeezing her tightly. We went back to the living room, and an episode had just started, so Gemma begged me to sit until that episode ended. I did, and when we got home, it was closed to one. We both had to work the next morning, but Gemma had to be there at seven. We had lazy sex. I knew it was because she had an earlier morning than me, so I took my one nut without a fight and then spooned with my baby as we both fell into a night of sleep.

15

MALICE

It was the first week of August, and we were getting married the last weekend of September. Grace and our moms had everything under control. There was no to-do list for me, although I wanted to be a part of the planning process, Dee-Dee quickly poured water on that flame. She made it clear that I'd just be in the way, and maybe she was right. I mainly wanted to do it to share this experience with my Princess, but I just let them have at it. She'd asked my input on some things but not much, so I just stopped sticking my nose in and concentrated on our honeymoon. Since Grace hadn't gone back to work yet, it was easy for us to take a week or two, and I definitely wanted to go somewhere romantic and out of the states; but when Grace told me that she didn't have a passport, I laughed out loud.

"Baby, you got to be joking, right?" I asked her, shaking my head in total disbelief.

"No, I am dead serious. I've never been out of the country."

"Okay, I get that, but you were never planning to leave? Even before we met, there was no girl's getaway in the works for you and your sisters? I mean, I am just shocked."

"I'm sure, but now I guess it is time to get one."

"It is, but unfortunately, it won't come soon enough. It takes some time for them to come back, so I will find us a beautiful place to honeymoon where there is no passport needed to go, I guess." My thoughts went to Florida or Hawaii, or even the Virgin Islands. After some internet surfing, I decided on Maui. It was beautiful enough and nice enough for my baby and me. So, I quickly reserved our room and then went hunting for two tickets. I hoped to get a good deal on our flights for the dates we were looking at, and I was so grateful that the prices seemed reasonable. Since it was the end of September, I figured that was basically an offseason, so I booked us two first-class tickets. Since my only two other tasks were my tux and rings, my to-do list was done. Gutta was hooking us up with the transportation as a gift, and I could not wait to give her my last name.

"Baby, can you come and help me, please?" I heard Grace call out. I was chillin' on the sofa, watching my favorite movie, *The Warriors*. It was a classic, and my brothers and I would watch it over and over as kids; that movie never got old to me.

"Sure babe," I said, tossed the remote, and then stood. I went over to help her with a few bags. "Baby, what is all of this?"

"Stuff for the wedding. I need to work on the centerpieces for the wedding."

I tilted my head. "Baby, you plan to do them all by yourself?" I asked her. She had a lot of stuff, so I wondered would she be overwhelmed.

"Yes, baby. I don't work anymore, and I know how to make them. I know exactly how I want them, so I am the best person to do it," she said.

"Okay, so I guess you want all of these bags in your studio?"

"I do," she smiled, and I leaned in to kiss her lips. She looked pretty that day, and I made sure to tell her that. Once I got all the bags in her studio, we headed back to the main living area, and she went to start dinner. I went to sit, and as soon as I pressed play, she called out my name. I closed my eyes for a moment and laughed to myself. I knew she would do that.

"Yes, Princess," I said, pretending to be annoyed.

"Can you come over and sit while I cook?"

"Babe, I am watching *The Warriors*," I whined.

"I know, but I have something I want to discuss with you. It won't take long, I promise." I faked a sigh and walked over like a sad kid. "Man, stop it and have a seat. You have seen that movie a million times."

I laughed as I took a seat. "I know, babe, I am just playing. What's on your mind, Juicy?"

"Well, I've been giving it some thought on what I want to do career-wise," she said, putting the cutting board down on the island.

"Okay, what is going on in that pretty little head of yours?"

"I think I want to open up a little studio. I mean, I am not sure what to call it, but one of those places where folks can come paint and sip wine. I can host the sessions and do something like poetry night, comedy, and host authors and things like that."

"Okay, that sounds great, baby... I mean, that is a fantastic idea. You are an awesome artist, so it would be fun for you to do something like that."

"Yes, it would be, but I am not business savvy like you. I don't know or have a clue about how to start a business."

"Well, lucky for you, I do. I can talk to my brothers, tell them what your vision is, and all we have to do is find a great spot, come up with a name, and then pretty much everything else is a walk in the park."

"Well, I want to call it Cocktails & Canvases, but how easy is easy? I don't have millions saved, Malice."

"Well, luckily, you don't need millions to open a business baby, and don't worry, we will figure out all the details, and I got you baby. Rel is a genius, as you know, when it comes to construction, so the best location is the key. And once we do that, if the space is affordable, we lease it or buy it. Either way, I will make it happen for you love."

Her face lit up, and a huge smile spread across her pretty red lips. She hurried around and hugged me tightly around the neck and kissed me. "I love you so much, Malice, and thank you for always doing everything within your power to make me happy."

"It is always a pleasure, Juicy, now may I please go back to my beer and movie?"

"Yes, you may, my love," she said, releasing the super-tight grip that she had on me. I went back to the sofa, and when I touched my once cold beer, it was now room temperature. I asked my baby to bring me another, and she did. I got back to my movie, thinking of the plans for my future wife and me. If my brothers and I could put our heads and resources together with Grace's ideas, there was no way we could not have her business opened within a few months. I smiled. Yep, I would find a way to give my baby exactly what she wanted.

❧ 16 ❧

GRACE

Time had just flown by, and it was the night before my
wedding. I was a lot calmer than I thought I'd be but so
damn anxious. Before meeting the girls at Chasity Rules,
Gloria Jean, Delilah, and I went by the church and reception hall
again. Once everything looked as perfect as we could get it that night,
they rushed me off to meet the girls. Delilah was not too happy that
we were having the wedding at my church at first, but she figured that
that would be my choice since that was my church home, and Malice
never attended service at her church since he was a teen. I called
Malice as soon as I got into his SUV. I had so many things in the back
for the next day, and all he had was the rings and his tux to transport,
so he cranked up the Caddy. I knew that was his baby, and he hardly
ever drove it; but his words were, "I will not be caught dead crammed
into a tiny ass Buick Encore." He would always tease that he'd have to
rip out the front seat and sit in the back just to have enough legroom.
He was right, my little ride was large enough for Bistro and me, so
after we return from our honeymoon, we would car shop for me a
larger vehicle.

When I told Malice about my business idea, I thought for sure he'd
wait until after the wedding to get on top of that, but I was wrong.

Within the next week, he and Rel were showing me different properties in popular booming areas that were for lease and sale. I found a spot that I loved and thought the place would be perfect because the bonus was a kitchen and a walk-in fridge and freezer. After seeing it in a prime location, the prospect of maybe serving finger foods made me more than interested in that place. It would need some minor upgrades and a cashier's station, but it was perfect.

My awesome, super talented, soon to be brother-in-law Rel insisted that it would be better for us to buy versus lease. After he gave it a thorough inspection, he estimated it to be worth less than 20K of what the seller was asking. He wasn't a real estate agent, but he knows the biz, so he negotiated the price down to over 40K of what they were asking; and before I knew it, my future husband came home with documents for me to sign. I kindly asked him to explain, and to put it simply, he was the financer to my new business. The deed and the ownership would be all mine, but the financial side, meaning the mortgage or purchase of the place, would be his. Rel estimated the 20K changes and renovations to be close to 10K. Since he was on the loan side of things, he put the expenses towards something business-related, and blah, blah, blah, meaning we would not have to pay a dime of that for me to open the doors. I stared at Malice, wondering if the words he was saying to me were make-believe, but then he said, "Juicy, do you follow everything I am saying?" I nodded yes because I did follow what he was telling me, but it was all so damn un-fucking-believable.

"I heard every word you have said, but I still can't believe that you and Rel have done this and got the space so damn quickly. I honestly thought this would be in motion after we exchanged vows, but you Wilkerson men stay busy."

He laughed lightly. "We are all family and all business. When I met with my brothers with the idea, all three were on board, Grace, so we moved forward. We won't and may never sit on something good. Like next year, Rel plans to expand Chasity Rules. Don't tell her please, but he has already found a location, and he wants to give her something big, Juicy, where she can do massages, facials, and so many other things that you women like to treat yourself to."

"First, how does Rel know that is what Chas wants?"

"Really, babe, are you seriously asking that? He knows his wife, just like I know you. They communicate, and he listens, so please keep this between us, okay. We are investing in a larger, more luxurious Chasity Rules."

"Where is it, baby?"

"Nope, nope, oh no. I've already said too much."

"Babe, come on, your secret is safe with me."

"I know my love, but you will just have to wait and see."

"Fine, so where do I sign?" I asked. He pointed out the lines that I needed to sign, and within a week before my wedding, I was signing documents to legalize my business name as *Cocktails & Canvases.* I was overjoyed, and I was happy beyond words.

"So, Miss Grace, are you nervous at all about exchanging vows with Superman?" Legacy asked. She was now working at Chasity Rules after Chas said she had to offer her the lowest booth rent possible to leave Sassy Styles.

"I am not nervous at all, I am just anxious to be Mrs. Wilkerson on paper. I mean, I was already his wife the night I gave him my body, love, and heart, but tomorrow after the worldly traditions, I will be addressed properly as his wife, not his live-in, or his fiancée, or just his woman. I will be respected as his wife," I answered. I was sitting in Chas' chair, and the usual stylists, Carmen and Loren, were there to pre-glam us up for the next day.

"I know that is real," Gemma said. "I know I will be next. Royal and I have just grown so damn close, it's like I have to pinch myself every once in a while. I mean, he is on my damn nerves sometimes with trying to control me and tell me what to do, but I be like, 'Royal, Boris Jackson is still alive, and breathing and you ain't him, so fuck what you talkin' about?'" she said and then sipped her wine. "And then I be a good lil girlfriend and do what the fuck he told me to do," she said, and we all burst into laughter. Tori laughed so hard, she started to choke on her damn champagne.

"Gem, your ass is so damn special," Gabby said.

"Girl, y'all don't know. Royal might not be as giant as Malice over-sized ass or as built as Rel and Gutta, but babbbbbyyyyy, let me tell you that baby Wilkerson got dick for muthafuckin' days, and I be on that shit, like..." Gemma said, getting her animated ass up to demonstrate. We were all used to her, giving us a visual, so we all laughed and high fived when she squatted and bounced like she was really riding Royal's dick. The girls roared with cheers, and I got a good laugh watching my baby sister carry on and talk about Royal. The last two people on earth that I thought would get together came together, and at that moment, I realized that love was stronger than pride.

"So Gem, if Royal proposes to you, what will you say?" I asked.

"Hell, fuck to the yeah, baby. I'd give that pussy slayer kids or even triplets if that is what he wanted," Gemma continued. I knew part of what she was saying was the champagne talking, but I also knew she had fallen in love with a Wilkerson man, just like Gabby, Chas, and I had.

"I guess we better stop looking at baby Royal like he a baby, the way you cutting up in here," Gabby said.

"Yeah, stop it because ain't nothing little about my man hunty, for real," Gemma said with a circle snap. My girls and I did what we did for the last two weddings and chilled without clubs and strippers. We went back to Chas' place, and the men were at Gabby's. I had no idea who had GiGi and EJ. I just knew I was grateful to have my girls. Chas was a great host and friend, and the next morning, there was a cook at her place to prepare our breakfast. Even though I thought it was a bit early to be drinking, mimosas were served, and after my shower, we had a group prayer. We all took turns telling the Father what we were grateful for, and after the prayer, we lounged a little, talking and laughing. The day was perfect and going so great, and when it was time for make-up, I felt so good.

Malice was my match, my mate, and my forever, and I could not wait to see him at the altar. After my make-up, it was like everything moved in fast forward because before I knew it, I was standing in front of the church filled with people with my king. I tried to keep it together during the ceremony, but tears of joy just kept falling from my eyes. My gentle giant kept blotting my face with his handkerchief, and I kept a bright smile on my face. After we jumped the broom, I was finally Mrs. Michael Jamil Wilkerson. I was over the moon with joy, and when we were at the receiving line, I had a smile plastered on my face that could not be removed. Standing next to my man made me feel like the most blessed woman in the world, and inwardly, I continued to send praises up to The Most High for our union. I was happier that day than I had ever remembered being happy in my entire life.

For so long, I never thought I'd find love, and to actually have a wedding so beautiful was only a fantasy or dream for so long, and I still could not believe all of this was actually happening to me. The man of my dreams, meaning I didn't have to settle for one thing when it came to Malice. He was everything I envisioned, and everything about him was all right. I would be a business owner soon, and I had my family, my life was pretty damn great, and I was indeed humbly grateful.

✿ 17 ✿

ROYAL

I sat there, eyeing my baby as she danced with her sisters on the floor. She and her girls were having a ball at the reception, and it just made me, and my brothers sit back and watch them as they took turns in the circle, doing silly dances and dropping it low. Chas and Gemma were the two that dropped it the lowest to the floor, but even in her wedding dress, my new sister-in-law Grace managed to get low and work her ample hips. Gabby did her dance, jamming too, but Gutta confirmed that he had already told her that she could only drop it low to the floor for him alone, so we all knew why she refrained from turning out the dance floor like my baby and Chas.

Rel, like me, said that Chas was going to always do whatever she felt, so even if he had told her to not drop it low, she would have done that shit anyway, so he just let her do her thang. Shit, Gemma may have cuss me out if I dared to tell her how to do anything, so I just watched my baby get her groove on. Men were eyeing my baby, but I was confident, so that shit didn't bother me one bit.

"So, baby bro, what's the budget?" Rel asked me. I didn't want to take my eyes off of Gemma, but I turned to him.

"What? What are you talking about, big bro?" I questioned, confused.

"The ring budget, dude?" Malice added.

"Yes, we know you are next, so let us help you get the perfect ring," Gutta said.

"I honestly don't know. I mean, what's appropriate?"

"Nothing less than 5K, bro," Rel, said.

"Easy," I said. I'd spring for 10K, that wouldn't set me back at all.

"You sure you ready to do this?" Malice said.

I eyed my baby, laughing with her sisters, and the look on her beautiful face as she enjoyed herself gave me joy, so I nodded. "I am one-million percent sure."

"Say no more. Monday, meet me at my place around noon. I will have my jeweler there with a spread to choose from," Rel said.

"Bet," I said, giving my brother a Wilkerson's handshake. It was our handshake since I was old enough to shake hands, and then we all decided to go join our ladies on the floor. I danced behind my baby, holding her close, and she smelled so fucking amazing. I caressed her skin as we danced, and I just wanted to take her home and just hold her close. Yes, some pussy would have been sweet, but I just wanted to bond with her, vibe with her, and just express to her the things that I was feeling inside. She turned me on so fucking much, and it *had* to be love because I was on an emotional high. I felt territorial as if I did not one no other man even gazing at my baby, and that stood for something.

"Let's get out of here, baby," I whispered into her ear.

"We can't leave, Royal. Not until I see my sister off. My family would flip if I weren't here to see Gracie off, baby."

"Oh shit, babe, my bad. The send-off just completely slipped my mind," I said. I knew my folks would trip too if I disappeared before the married couple left.

"But if you wanna quickie, I know a spot," she said.

"Word?"

"Word. Our church members always, always use this facility for everything, so I know where we can sneak one in."

"You are a bad girl," I said.

"Like your ass is not a bad boy," she countered.

"You, right. I am," I breathed into her ear.

"Just let me leave out first. Go out the double doors and go to the right, all the way down to the last set of double doors on the left. It only has extra tables and chairs used for storage. We can get one in there," she said.

I was game. "Okay, lead the way, baby," I said. She slid out of my arms, and I went back over to our table. I watched her stop and exchange chit chat with guests and family, and two minutes after she walked through the double doors, I got up to follow her. I tried to make my exit quickly, but my drunk ass uncle Stew blocked my path.

"What it do, nephew?" he slurred.

"What's up, Unc? Err thang is good," I answered.

"I know that is real, nephew. I have been wanting to bring the old Lincoln to your spot and let you get her all nice and pretty."

"That is cool, Uncle Stew, anytime, you know I gotchu," I said and tried to move on, but he blocked my path.

"That's cool, nephew, but can I bring Lula Mae's car too? I mean, she treats her car like a damn dumpster."

"Unc, we good. I got her vehicle too." I said and slid on by him. I went out of the double doors and then followed my baby's instructions. When I walked into the doors, I didn't see her right away, but she called out my name in a soft whisper. I turned to my left to see my sexy ass lover leaning against the counter. I didn't hesitate to make my way over to her in a flash. Immediately, we kissed, and my hands were all over her body. I quickly found the path to her center and moved her panties to the side as I stroked her bulb with the tip of my finger. She moaned and licked my lips, and that shit turned me all the way on. I went down and kissed her center, allowing my tongue to lap up her juices that her center released. She never had any trouble getting wet for me, and my dick throbbed in my pants at the thought of how wet and tight her pussy would be, and I wanted to plunge inside of her.

"Condoms, baby, do you have a condom?" she panted as I licked my way up to her tongue. I had sucked and licked on her clit and opening, now I wanted to just push my dick inside of her.

"No, Gem, but I swear I am safe. I am clean," I said and then looked into her eyes. She stared at me for a few moments, and then she opened wider for me. I rubbed the head of my dick against her opening, and when she gripped my ass, pulling me into her, I went all the way in. Her silky tunnel felt so fucking good that I moaned louder than she did as I enjoyed every damn stroke. I pushed and pulled in and out of her heat, and my dick was in pussy bliss. She felt so damn good that I swear my moans were just as loud as hers. I had never once penetrated a woman without the plastic, and Gemma was my first. Before I could stop, my body betrayed me, and I nutted all up in her wetness. My body spasmed, and I almost felt paralyzed from the nut. I did all I could to keep from screaming like a bitch. Gemma had locked me down, and even though my brothers said 10k or less for a ring, I'd drain my entire account for her.

"Baby, are you good?" I asked.

"More than good, baby, and I can't wait to get home, so I can ride your dick and cum again," she cooed.

"That sounds so good to me, beautiful," I said, pulling out. My dick was good and shiny with our juices, but I pulled up my pants and boxers anyway. I kissed my baby ten times before we made our exit. We both headed to the bathroom, and I grabbed a few paper towels and wet them down with water before I went into my stall. I wiped my dick down with those paper towels, and then I took a piss. My dick was more than satisfied but ached for more. I could not get enough of Gemma, and I hoped that the married couple would soon make their exit so we can send them off, and I could get home to my baby.

Gemma

It had been a week since the wedding and nonstop sex with Royal and I. We had been at my place for the last few days, and since we were hosting game night with his friends, we were at his place. It was kinda strange spending time with other couples that were not my sisters and their mates, but Royal's friends were cool, and I finally got to meet Tas' live-in girlfriend. She was super cute in my opinion, but that didn't stop Tas from cheating on her every chance he got. I didn't like that about Tas, but he wasn't my man, so it wasn't my damn business.

The games were underway, and the shit-talking was on and popping. We played in teams: the girls against the guys, then couples against couples in Pictionary, and by the end of the night after everyone else had gone, Tas, Lisa, Royal, and me played spades. It was after two when they finally left since Lisa had helped me to tidy up. I was exhausted, but my man wanted sex. "Not tonight, baby, please... I am tired as hell," I grumbled as he massaged my tits from behind. I felt his erection pressed against my ass, but I was too tired to move.

"Just lie here, baby, you don't have to do anything. Just let me slide in baby," he said, still trying to complete his sexual mission. I wanted to, but I was so tired.

"I promise in the morning, baby," I said, resisting.

"Baby, you can't expect me to fall asleep like this, can you? My dick his harder than a muthafucka, baby, come on, I promise I won't hold back. I will let my nut bust quick tonight, I won't make it last," he said. Royal could go for hours if I let his ass, and that night, I didn't have enough energy to just go his one round. One round with him could be another forty to forty-five damn minutes, but I gave in to my lover.

"Okay, okay, okay, but you better not take forever to bust, man. I need sleep like nobody's business," I said, turning over onto my back. I let him pull away my panties, and then I sat up and pulled my tank over my head. He started kissing me, making his way down to my nipples, and that was all it took for me to be fully aroused by Royal. He was a nipple pleaser, and the magic his tongue would do to my center had me woken all the way up. By the time I climaxed, I was ready for him to work my center over with his harden masterpiece, so I paused, reaching over to get the box of rubbers from his nightstand drawer.

I pulled the box out, and when only one condom fell from the box, I shook that shit to make sure the box was definitely empty. When I realized it was, I snapped. "Royal, what the fuck?!" I blasted.

"Baby, what is it? What's wrong?"

"You fucked another bitch?" I yelled, getting up from the bed with the quickness. I damn near knocked the lamp off of the nightstand, trying to turn it on.

"Gem, baby, what in the fuck are you talking about? NO! What kinda question is that?"

"Don't play games with me, muthafucka! There were three condoms in this got-damn box the last time we fucked here at your got-damn place... now, there is only one. Where in the fuck are the other two condoms?" I yelled loud as fuck. My hands were shaking, and my heart started to fucking beat fast as hell. I just knew there was no possible way that Royal had cheated on me.

"Baby, you gotta be mistaken because I ain't fucking with no one else but you. I love you, and you know good and got-damn well that ain't nobody fucking around on you, Gemma... that shit if fucking absurd!" he countered, getting up from the bed. A sheer look of panic was written all over his face, but I was no damn fool. I knew without a shadow of a doubt that there were three fucking condoms in that box the last I checked. We now had condoms at my place, so I knew he hadn't pulled a condom out of his pocket when we screwed at my place.

"Then, where are the fucking rubbers, Royal?" I asked him. At that point, my eyes started to well, and my lips began to tremble.

He moved over to the nightstand and snatched the drawer open, and he moved shit around like they were in there. "They have to be in here, baby, or you had to miscount because I fucking swear to you that I ain't had nobody up in here," he said and started looking around the side of the bed and then underneath. He moved the covers around as if they may have fallen somehow in the dark from the box, and I wanted to punch him in the back of his muthafuckin' head for pretending to look for two whole damn condoms.

"You know what? Stop, just stop!" I blared because the fake ass attempt to find the condoms was pissing me the fuck off. "Just fucking stop. You are a fucking cheating ass, bitch ass liar, and I cannot believe I trusted your ass," I said, going for my clothes.

"Hold the fuck on Gemma! Baby, please. I swear on my life... I swear on *everything* that I didn't cheat on you... you have to be mistaken, baby. I didn't do shit! I don't have a clue what the fuck happen to two damn rubbers... I promise you had to have miscounted,

Gem," he said, trying to stop me from putting on my clothes. He was visibly shaking, and so was I.

"Get your fucking hands off of me! I don't believe that bullshit and fuck no, I didn't miscount," I belted. I had to get the fuck away from him before things got physical because I wanted to beat the fuck out of him.

He went back to hunting for the missing condoms as if they were going to magically turn up while I gathered my shit. I slid my feet into my house shoes because I didn't have time to put on my Air Force Ones. I rushed to the door, but he was right on my heels.

"No, no, no, no, no, no, Gemma, baby, please wait. I don't know what the fuck is going on, and I can't let you leave like this baby... I love you, and I've been true blue wit you since day one. I love you... I mean, I *truly* love you, baby! And I did not cheat on you, Gemma... I didn't have a woman up in here."

"Liar!" I yelled. "If you can't tell me how two damn condoms magically vanished from that fucking box..." I yelled, pointing at his room. "We are *done*. I don't have time to deal with unfaithful muthafuckas like you. You said you loved me, you told me that you'd never do shit to hurt or disrespect me, but you fuck another bitch! I hope those two rounds were worth it!" I spat and snatched the door opened. I raced to my Audi and put the pedal to the medal to get the fuck away from his place. My eyes blurred as the tears began to pour. I had fallen for his ass, I mean *really* fallen for him. I liked men before Royal, even cared deeply, but he was the first to still my heart, and not even a year had gone by, and he cheated.

I continued to swipe my tears as I weaved in and out of traffic. Royal started to blow up my phone, and I kept hitting ignore. When I got home, he had called my cellphone maybe two dozen times, but I didn't answer. I got to my building, parked, and walked to the gate to unlock it. My hands trembled so bad that I had a hard time pushing the key into the lock. Once inside my building, I took the steps two by two, hurrying up to my unit. Since Royal had a key, I made sure I dead-bolted my top lock, so if he came by, he would be unable to get in. He sent me text after text after text, and I finally powered my phone completely off. It was after three a.m., but I went for the bottle of Ciroc. I took a couple of back to back shots as I cried so many tears. I was trying to figure out when did he make time for another woman? Then it was a no brainer because I worked a lot, had a night shift here and there, and often times pulled a double at the hospital, so he had plenty of time to fuck as many women as he wanted to.

Then I thought about the gorgeous chick that I saw him with in VIP that night, could it have been her? More tears. I thought about Mari, the way she always grinned in my man's face. I mean, she was kind enough to Gutta, Malice, and Rel, but it seemed she was always extra sweet to Royal. So many things danced around in my head, and I hated that he didn't value the relationship as much as I did. I mean, all the while, I thought we were on the road to engagement and even marriage like Gutta and Gabby, Rel and Chas, and Malice and Grace. I watched how they all treated their women like silk while my low-down dirty ass man stuck his dick in another or maybe even a few others. I was so heartbroken and sad. I wanted to call my sisters, but Grace was not coming home until Monday from her honeymoon, and I didn't want to wake Gabby or Chas at that hour, so I crawled into my empty bed and cried myself to sleep.

❧ 18 ❧

ROYAL

I called Gemma over and over and over and over again, and I knew that she wasn't going to answer. I kept texting her, telling her I had no idea what was going on or how on fucking earth could two damn condoms be gone from the box. When I first started fucking with Gemma, the box was damn near full, so I definitely wasn't keeping count, and I had no damn idea she was. But what I did know, she had to be off or drunk or just forgot because I had no damn clue how or what could have possibly happened. I had to figure out something because I bought Gemma a damn ring the day before, and I was waiting on Grace and Malice to return to pop the question. I wanted to surprise her in front of our family and friends, and now shit was all fucked up. I had to somehow convince her that I didn't do any dirty deeds with any other woman and that she was the only woman that I wanted. Giving her that ring had to make her see how serious I was about her and about us.

Once her phone started going straight to voicemail, I knew she had powered off her phone. I threw on some sweats, a hoodie, and my slides, and snatched up my phone and keys. I went into my room, opened my closet, went into the shoebox where I had her ring hidden, and grabbed my jacket. I dropped the ring in my inside pocket, and I raced out the door. I had to talk to her. I had to somehow make her think back to the last time we made love at my place to see if she could truly remember it being three condoms after we were done or three before we started. There had to be some kind of explanation, or else I'd lose Gemma for sure. I stopped at a stop sign and bam, the shit hit me. I had left Tas' ass at my crib one night when he wanted to smash some chick he had been stalking. I pulled out my phone and texted, **DUDE, DID YOU FUCKIN' USE TWO CONDOMS FROM MY DRAWER?**

I then put my foot on the gas to proceed, and all I heard was the loud boom that hit my driver's side door, and everything went black.

❧ 19 ❧

GEMMA

The next morning, the thunderous sounds banging on my damn door woke me. I looked at the clock, and it was only a little after six, and that meant I hadn't slept long. I knew it was Royal's ass, so I didn't budge. I shut my eyes, hoping he'd go away, but the pounding continued, so I threw the covers back and stomped to the door. "Go the fuck away because I'll call the law on your ass, Royal," I yelled.

"Gem, it's me, Gabby and Chas open up," my sister said.

I shook my damn head and let out a breath. That muthafucka woke my sister and Chas. The nerve of his cheating ass. I undid the locks and snatched the door opened. "Look, please don't come over here defending that muthafucka!" I blasted, but the looks of sadness on their faces and the way they looked a mess told me that they were not there to get Royal and me back together. Gabby looked as if she had been crying. "What, what is it, Gab? Is it momma, daddy? Grace, what in the hell is going on?" I quizzed.

"Gem, baby, you have to get dress, there has been an accident, honey," my sister said softly.

"What? Who? Gabby, what's going on?"

"It's Royal, Gem... he was in an accident, and he is at Mercy," Chas said, and my heart dropped into the pit of my damn stomach. My damn knees went weak, and I fell back against the wall. They hurried inside to help me. "Come on, Gem, we have to get you on some clothes."

"Is he okay?" I cried. Suddenly, my face was wet with my tears.

"We don't know, Gem. When we headed over here, he was in surgery. We tried calling your phone over and over."

"We, we, we, we... had a fight," I said, now sobbing. "I powered my phone off," I said, letting them guide me to my bedroom. I felt like I was in a daze, and suddenly, I felt so lightheaded. "I need to sit for a moment, Gab," I said, and they helped me over to the chair in my bedroom.

"Chas, get her some water, please," Gabby said. Chas nodded and was off. "Just breathe, Gem, just breathe. We are going to take you to the hospital, so we can see what is going on with him. The wreck was pretty bad, Gem... the other car hit his on the driver's side, and he was hurt really bad."

I heard her words, but then I heard sounds of cries come out of me that I had never heard before. I had worked in that ER for three years, and I had seen accident victims die, so I was inconsolable. Chas and Gabby gave me a few minutes to get myself together, and then I threw on something that was at the foot of my bed, and we went to the hospital. Everyone was there, and when I saw my mother, I ran into her arms and cried even harder. Her and my father held me close, and when I sat down, Royal's mom came to sit beside me. She didn't say anything; she just took my hand, and I held on to hers so tight. After three hours of prayers and waiting, the doctor finally came out. He explained that it was touch and go at that point. Royal had two broken legs, a minor concussion, and the impact caused minor damage to his lungs. He had an oxygen tube down his throat that the doctor said he'd keep in place for a couple of days, but he was breathing fine on his own. The doctor assured us that it was a very strong possibility that he would pull through entirely without any complications. Only his parents were allowed to see him, but since I knew Dr. Reed, he allowed me to go back after his parents had gone.

I was no stranger to the tubes and machines, but it broke my damn heart to see him like that. I touched his face, grabbed his hand, and then kissed his fingers. I knew he'd be out for a while because he was heavily sedated. I peeled off my hot ass jacket and hung it and my purse on the coat hook near the door. I slid the chair closer to his bed, and I sat down. "I know you thought to lie to me would make it okay, but it didn't. I was so angry and hurt for what you did, but none of that shit matters now, baby. I just want you to fight as hard as you can to keep breathing on your own for me. This machine will make breathing easier for you for a couple days, babe, but I know you are a strong man. You have Wilkerson blood running through your veins, and y'all are fighters, especially when it's for love. I forgive you baby for cheating and lying, okay. It hurts, but seeing you like this hurts more," I said, wiping my tears as they fell. I didn't want to leave his side, but I figured I'd go home, shower, and put on some comfy clothes while he was unaware that anyone was there.

I'd pack a bag because I'd be there with him until they let him go home, and no way I wasn't going to be there when he opened his eyes. I stopped at the nurse's station to let them know to call me immediately if anything changed with him. I knew the entire staff, so I knew they had my back. When I got out to the waiting room, Gabby and Gutta were still there waiting for me to take me home, and Tas was also still there. They all stood.

"How is he, Gem?" Gutta asked.

"The same Gutta. It will be a few days before we truly know anything, and as long as there are no infections, there should not be any complications. He will definitely be in a chair for a whole minute with both legs broken, but I will take care of him until he is fully recovered."

"We know sis," Gabby said, hugging me tightly.

"And if there is anything that you need, sis, I mean anything, don't hesitate?"

"Thanks, Gutta," I said and turned to Tas. "You may as well go home. Royal won't wake for a long while. They will have him heavily sedated for hours," I said to him.

"I know, but can I talk to you in private for a moment?"

"Sure," I said with a nod.

"We will pull the car up, Gem," Gutta said.

"Okay," I said. They left, and I turned back to Tas. "What's going on?"

"I wanted to talk to you before I left, but I couldn't say much in front of the family."

"Listen, Tas, I already know that Royal fucked around on me, and at this moment, I really don't give a shit about all of dat!" I spat. I knew it wasn't his fault that Royal cheated, but I didn't want him in my face defending his disloyalty to me.

"Hold... on, wait, Gemma, is that what Royal told you?"

"What do you mean?"

"Right before the accident this morning, Royal texted me this, and then I texted this back to him," he said, showing me his phone. "I thought I'd hear back from him, but I got a call from Rel saying that there was an accident," he said. I read the text that Royal had sent, and then read Tas reply – **YEAH, MAN DAMN, THAT NITE WHEN U LET ME AND OLE GIRL CHILL AT YO' SPOT WHEN U WENT OVER TO GEMS .... MY BAD, I 4GOT 2 TELL U.** Those words made my eyes burn because Royal had been telling the truth. "I wanted to say something earlier, but Lisa was here. Royal was always true blue with you, Gemma... he would never mess around on you, so I wanted to let you know that whatever you thought, it was me."

I wanted to slap him and myself. Him for being a whore and using my man's place to hook up with bitches behind Lisa's back, and myself for not trusting and believing my man. "Damn, Tas, fuck! Why didn't you just let him know? We got into a big ass fight because of fucking missing condoms. And my man is all fucked up right now because he was out on the road this morning trying to convince me that he was telling the truth. I mean got'damn Tas, grow the fuck up, and stop dogging Lisa the fuck out! If your cheating ass had never taken condoms from the box, Royal and I would be home right now, and none of this shit would have happened," I cried. I couldn't stand his ass, and when he tried to put his arms around me to console me, I slapped his hands away. "Don't you fucking touch me," I hissed. Deep down, I knew that God was in control and everything that was happening was His will, that is why it did. However stupid ass couldn't keep his dick in his pants, Tas should have just told Royal, and we would still be at his house... in his bed.

"Gemma, I am so sorry," Tas said, and I was sure he was, but that shit changed nothing.

"What the fuck ever nigga. You need to go home and tell Lisa why your best friend almost died this morning!" I barked and then walked away from him. I got into the backseat of Gutta's SUV, and I cried the entire ride back to my house. I assured Gabby that I'd be okay and that I was just going to shower and change and head back to Mercy, so she allowed me to go up by myself. I showered and thought back on the events that transpired at Royal's and wondered if he had told me that Tas took two condoms, would I have believed that. The answer to that was *hell no*, so the events of the night before may have played out the exact same way. *"Please forgive me, God, for not believing him when he told me that he never cheated. I should have trusted him,"* I cried. I got out of the shower, dressed, packed a bag, and headed back. I let my supervisor know that I would need a few days off, at least until Royal was breathing on his own and moving around.

I knew in about three or four days, he most likely will have the oxygen tube removed, but it was always that small percentage that had rare complications, so I still prayed a lot. The next day, Royal opened his eyes, and I smiled. I was there when the doctor explained to him what had happened, and he was able to nod his head. The doctor asked a few questions that required a *yes* answer, and each time Royal nodded his head, I released a deep breath. As soon as the doctor left, I was right there by his side.

The doctor said that he would go and call Royal's mom and dad, and then he reminded me again that Royal would pull through just fine. "Hey baby," I said, and I could see that he was still a bit groggy. His eyes danced, though, so that indicated that he knew who I was. "Can you hear me okay, baby?" I asked, and he nodded. "I know you have a million and one questions, but first I want to tell you that you are going to be just fine. Your injuries were significant, but the surgery went so well that in a couple of days, that uncomfortable tube will be out, and you will be able to breathe on your own. You might need therapy to walk once your legs are healed, but you are going to make it through it all, baby, and I will be right here by your side." He nodded, and a tear fell from his eyes. I wiped his face. "No baby, don't do that okay," I said, and another one fell, causing me to cry too. "Listen, I love you, and I know you didn't cheat on me. Tas told me the truth about the condoms, and I am so fucking sorry for not believing you," he nodded again. I leaned in and put so many kisses on his face, and I made sure that he was comfortable and not in any pain.

His parents came, and then the rest of the family arrived. I let everyone go see him because only two could go back at a time. When Malice and Grace walked in, I ran to hug them both. They had landed, and Gutta brought them straight to the hospital. They had known about the accident but couldn't make it back any earlier, so they both had tons of questions. The entire family stayed for hours, all taking turns going back to visit with Royal. When Tas walked in with Lisa, I gave him a look before I walked over to greet them. I gave Lisa a tight hug, and then even though I still despised Tas, I hugged him too.

"I told Lisa the truth, and I am so sorry, Gemma. This was a hard wake up call for me, and I am sorry that I caused drama with you and Royal. I feel horrible about the entire ordeal. You gotta know that I didn't mean for any of this to happen."

I believed him, and although it would take me a while to like him again, I forgave him. "I accept your apology Tas."

"Thank you, Gemma," he said. Lisa had already taken a seat by my sister. "So, she forgave you, huh?"

"Yeah, she is a good woman, and I did think that she'd leave, but I am grateful that she didn't."

"Well, I hope you don't take her kindness for weakness but do right by her because we can only take so much. And if you honestly don't want to lose her, get your shit together."

"I hear ya, Gem." I went back over and sat by Lisa. She was sweet, and I was good with her being in our circle if she wanted to be. The waiting room stayed filled with our family and friends until visiting hours were over. I stayed with Royal all night again, and the next day, I told the CNA that I would bathe him. He was awake when I did, and when I touched his dick to wipe it down, it got semi-erect. Royal still had a catheter in there, so I said, "You better calm down baby because that catheter is in there, and a woody might hurt you, baby." I felt his body move as if he was laughing, and I couldn't wait until the tubes were out.

20

ROYAL

My voice was so scratchy when they removed the tube from my throat. I swallowed, and my throat hurt, so I rubbed my neck.

"Your throat will be sore for a couple of days, Raphael, so don't worry, the nurse can give you something for that. We are just happy that you can breathe on your own. The puncture was small but large enough for us to go in and repair it. It will be a rough six to eight weeks for you, but you should recover just fine without extra oxygen," the doctor said as he examined me. He gave me several instructions as he listened with his stethoscope, and I did whatever he said to do. It was challenging to breathe in deeply as I wanted to, but I tried as hard as I could. It sounded like I was wheezing a lot, but with my injury, I knew that was to be expected. I was just so glad to have that damn tube out of my damn throat. He explained that the catheter would be in for a while longer until I was able to fully move around. I wondered just how long it would be before I was back to my old self again. Once the doctor finally vacated my room, my baby was right there.

"Hey, beautiful," I said hoarsely. My voice was jacked up, and my mouth was dry as hell.

"Hey baby, how are you feeling?" she smiled at me.

"Just thirsty," I said.

"Let me get you some ice chips because I don't think you should be drinking water yet," Gemma said and left the room. When she came back, she fed me a few of the chips, and the coolness felt good inside of my mouth. She leaned in and kissed my lips, and I smiled. I knew my breath had to be funky as fuck, but I guess she didn't mind.

"I heard everything you've said the last few days, baby," I managed to say.

"I'm glad, and I am sorry," she said again for the hundredth time.

"Baby, no, you don't owe me any more apologies. We are good, and I don't remember much about the accident, I just remembered trying to get to you."

She smiled. "I love you so much, Royal, and I thank God over and over again for not taking you away from me. If you had died that night after how I treated, you and after all the mean things I said to you..."

"Shhhhh, baby, no, don't do that. I am here, and this right here is going to be okay... and I am going to heal, and then I'm going to marry you, and we are going to have pretty kids," I teased. And that made her smile so brightly. "We have been through a lot, and we are going to be okay," I said and then remembered her ring. "Oh, shit, where are my clothes from that night?"

"They were destroyed in the O.R. They had to cut your clothes away," she said.

"And my personal stuff like my watch, my wallet, my phone? My jacket? I was wearing a jacket," I said.

"I think Rel or Gutta took that bag home, baby, why? What's wrong?"

"I need your phone, call my brothers now," I said in a panic. I had just paid close to 6K for her ring, and I prayed that it was with my stuff. She handed me the phone. "Gutta, man," I said in my raspy ass voice.

"Royal, is that you, bro?"

"Yes, where are you, big bro?"

"We are all on our way to the hospital. Mom called and said the tube was out, so everyone is headed that way."

"Please tell me that you have my wallet and personal items. I had valuables on me that night," I said, and I knew he had to hear the fear in my voice. At least I hoped because I was hoarse as hell.

"Yeah, I got it, including the ring," he said. I let out a breath, and at that moment, it honestly pained me to breathe.

"Thank God," I said and handed Gemma the phone. I had to take slow breaths and calm all the way down because my entire chest was burning like a bitch.

"Listen, thanks, Gutta. I got to go because he is having trouble breathing," she said. I guess my expressions let her know that I was in some sort of pain. Gemma put the phone down and got closer to aid me. She hit the button and sat me up even higher than what I already was, and that gave me some instant relief, but not completely. "Just take small breaths baby until you can get back to a normal breath. Don't try to suck in too much air, okay. Although it feels like you are not getting enough air, you are okay, baby, just slow and easy," she coached, and then I began to relax. The burning started to subside, and the calmer I got, the less pain I felt. When my breathing was steady, I was able to suck in a little more air at a time, and I was grateful that she was there to calm me down. "Is that better, baby?" she asked softly, and I nodded. Gemma reclined me a little and gave me another kiss on my lips and then my face. "You can't get too excited right now. If you feel like you can't hardly breathe, press this button to sit all the way up and take in small breaths until you can take in larger ones. It will be like this for a little while, but it will get better, I promise."

I nodded again. Before long, my family was there. I don't know what Gemma did, but they were all packed inside of my room. It was so good to have everyone there, and I loved the love they all showered on me. When Gutta slipped me the ring box, he winked at me. Since our closes and the immediate family was in the room, I gave Gutta a nod.

"Hey everyone, listen up, our little bro has something to say, and since y'all know his voice is jacked up, we got to be extra quiet," he joked, and everyone laughed. "Gem, get over her lil sis... baby Royal got something he wants to say," he added.

She came over and stood beside me, and I took her hand. "Since everyone is here, I want to take a moment to let everyone know just how much I love this mean ass woman," I said.

"Ralph," Dee-Dee said with a look.

"My bad momma, but she is... but that is one of the things I like about her. She is fierce but kind. Mean but also loving, and she is just right for me."

"Awwww, babe," Gemma said.

"Hold on babe, I'm not done."

"Okay," she said with a neck twist. Everyone laughed again.

"I wanted to do this someplace fancy with the family or somewhere romantic, but things just kinda went left, so I am asking you to be my wife," I said and pulled the ring box from underneath my covers, and she covered her mouth. I opened it, and a tear fell from her eyes before I could get the ring out of the box. I held it up and ask, "Please marry, babe?"

She whispered a soft *yes* with a head nod. I put the ring on her finger, and she leaned in and kissed me, funky breath and all. I wished someone had given me a damn mint or something, but oh well. Our families cheered and congratulated us. A month after I got home, Gemma moved into my place. She took a leave of absence to take care of me, and she indeed took care of me. After both casts were off, Gemma basically became my physical therapist, and she literally nursed me back to good health. She took care of me every single day and never once left my side, and I was genuinely grateful to have Gemma as my lover, friend, and new bride.

EPILOGUE

One Year Later
Gabby

We were all at Chas and Rel's gender reveal party. They had gone through infertility, and the issues that Chas had caused her to have invitro, and they were now having triplets. They had implanted three embryos to increase their chances, and all three survived, so they were going to have a house full, to begin with. Chas vowed that would be the only three that they'd have and Rel second that. There were three cakes on the table, and everyone was so excited as we all watched them cut into the first one. When they pulled out the slice, it was blue, and everyone applauded. They cut into cake number two and again pulled away another blue slice, more applause, and whistles. I could see that Chas was happy, but I knew she wanted a little girl too, so I watched my friend cross her fingers as they cut into the third and final cake. When they pulled out a slice of pink cake, my best friend screamed in excitement. Rel pulled her into his arms, giving her a tight hug and a big kiss.

The music came back on, and then we got back to having fun. I was so happy to see my parents dancing and having fun, and even Dee-Dee danced with Samson with a huge grin plastered on her face. Royal was swaying, holding my sister tight. We all loved to see that he was finally walking without a cane for help or support. He and Gemma tied the knot a couple of months ago in Vegas, pissing Gloria Jean and Delilah off, but they wanted to do what made them both happy. By the end of the night, our husbands decided they wanted to hang out, doing whatever they had planned for the night. Since Chas was five months and larger than life, no way she was going out, so the girls decided to meet up back at my place. We were all chattering about our men, marriage, and the future when Grace tapped her glass.

"Excuse me, ladies, but I have news," she said.

"You do? Well, let's hear it, Missy," Gemma said.

"Well, I am not sure if you guys have noticed that I've only drunk the Apple Cider today and no wine or champagne..." she said.

"Ummm, we hadn't, but since you mentioned it," I said.

"We, I, didn't want to steal any of Chas' glory today by telling the family at the gender reveal party, but Malice and I will soon be parents too. I am pregnant!" she shared, and we all cheered.

"I didn't even know that you two were trying," Chas said as she hugged Grace.

"We were not, but I guess the pill is not the right type of birth control for me because I forgot to take them one too many times. So, after this baby, we have to find another method."

"Welp, that is more wine for Gab and me," Gemma said.

"Right," I agreed. "I mean, I love my husband, and I love lil GiGi, but I am so not ready to do that shit all over again. Plus, with Chas having three, and now Grace having one too, there will be enough Wilkerson babies to occupy us all for a while."

"Sho Nuff," Gemma said. "So is Malice happy?"

"Is he. I kept telling his ass not to run his mouth earlier. He wanted to make a big announcement."

"Y'all should have. Rel and I would not have minded if you shared your good news with the entire family."

"It's cool... we'll share it on Sunday at Sunday dinner."

"Well, I hope Royal doesn't get baby fever because I am not ready."

"What if he is, though?"

Crazy ass Gemma stood and started to do her famous horse-riding motion. "All I have to do is this, and he will go back to speaking in *Gemma*," she said, and we roared in laughter. She was a clown.

We chatted for a little while longer. When my husband called and said he was on his way home and Rel was on his way to pick up Chas, Gemma and Grace left. I kissed Chas goodnight, and my husband and I headed upstairs. I told him about Grace and Malice's news, and as soon as I did that, he asked me for another baby. Shit! That was my first thought, but once Gutta slid inside of me, that went out the window. His dick was so damn good, that day I would have given him whatever the hell he wanted, and three months later, we had conceived again.

Chas babies were born healthy and beautiful. Malice and Grace had a little boy, and two months after I gave birth to my baby boy, Gemma and Royal finally announced that they were pregnant. In the end, I gave Gutter three kids, two boys, and one girl. Chas and Rel stopped at the triplets, and Malice and Grace stopped at two sons. Gemma and Royal ended up with two, a boy and a girl, and we all lived blissful married lives with our Wilkerson men!

THE END!

NOTE FROM THE AUTHOR

Thanks, everyone, for your support and love. If you loved this story, please do me a solid by posting a review. This contest will be a little different because I need to boost reviews, so screenshot your posted review and email it to annablackgive-aways@gmail.com, and you will be entered into a drawing to win some cold hard cash! That's right, I am giving away 25.00 bucks to four lucky winners. Contest begins October 7th and ends October 28th just so more readers can have a chance to enter. Drawing will be on October 31st, so if you want an opportunity to win. Remember, you must screenshot your actual posted review to qualify. Also, check out Masterpiece Readers group on Facebook for our October contest. First place is 500.00, second place is 100 and third place is 50.00. Good luck, ladies & gents.

Happy Reading!

ABOUT THE AUTHOR

Anna Black is a native of Chicago and the bestselling author of the I'm Doin' Me series. Her desire to become a published author didn't develop until her late twenties, and she didn't take her writing seriously until several close friends and family members encouraged her to go for it. In November 2009, Anna became a bestselling author for her debut release, Now You Wanna Come Back, within a matter of weeks.

She has since released over two dozen novels, short stories, and collaborations. As she forges her path to success, her goal is to offer page-turning tales to her many followers and fans. This award-winning author currently lives in Texas with her daughter Tyra, and her adorable dogs Jaxson and Jasmine.

Please contact me at www.annablackbooks.com, info@annablackbooks.com, or on all social media sites.